The Case of the Artist's Mistake

Sweetbrier Inn Mysteries
Book Two

Jan Drexler

Published by Swift Wings Press

Keystone, South Dakota

ISBN-13 979-8-9861378-2-7

Cover design by Hannah Linder

www.hannahlinderdesigns.com

Edited by Beth Jamison

To my daughter Carrie,
whose value is far above rubies

Soli Deo Gloria

One

"It looks like you need this," Becky said as she thrust a mug into my hand.

I breathed in the coffee's aroma, feeling the brain cells wake up.

"Thanks. I stayed up too late last night finishing that new murder mystery." I sipped the hot liquid.

Becky went back to filling muffin tins with batter. "Did you solve the case before the end of the book?"

"Of course." I took another sip. "What's on the menu for this morning?"

In the four weeks since Becky had accepted the job as our cook at Rose's Sweetbrier Inn, she had settled into the job like she had been born to it.

"A baked omelet and these blueberry muffins. I also made that fruit slush recipe Gran got from the Amish tourists last week." She slid the muffin tin into one of the ovens and set the timer. "We'll see how it goes before I make it a permanent part of the menu."

"You're using the guests for guinea pigs?"

"Don't worry. I tried it at Gran's and it's delicious. The guests will love it."

The caffeine began to clear the fog in my brain. "Run through this weekend's events for me one more time. Is there anything our guests will be interested in?"

"It's Paragon Days." Becky took the batter bowl to the sink and rinsed it with the sprayer arm. "It's a big thing. Folks come from all over the Hills for the parade on Saturday and the Ice Cream Social on Sunday evening."

"It sounds like something out of a Norman Rockwell painting."

"Every Memorial Day weekend." Becky grinned at me as she refilled her coffee cup. "Which float did you decide to join?"

"Me?"

"Sure. You have your pick. The church has a float, and Gran's Café is always a good one." She stirred sugar and cream into her cup, then her eyebrows went up. "Hey, maybe this year the inn should have a float."

"I don't know the first thing about building a parade float. And didn't you say the event is tomorrow morning? When would either of us have time to work on it?"

Becky slumped against the counter. "You're right." Then her face brightened. "But we can start making plans for next year, can't we? Do you think Rose would pay for some decorations?"

I laughed at Becky's enthusiasm. "We can discuss that after this weekend is over. Are you still planning to go into town with me today? I want to distribute those new brochures."

"Let's have lunch at the café, then we'll do the tour. Most of the seasonal stores are open now. Except..." She left the word hanging when the oven timer rang.

I waited while she took out the casserole and set it on the counter. "Except what?"

"Have you seen the new art gallery yet?"

"The storefront across from Gran's Café? Don't you like it?"

She poured herself a fresh cup of coffee. "Hey, I like purple as much as the next person. Maybe more. But her place is-"

"Funky? Groovy? Way out there?"

"Yeah. Like something from the hippie-sixties. And the woman who runs it is driving everyone in town crazy."

"She's new. Maybe people need to get used to her."

Becky gave me a sideways look. "You haven't met her, have you?"

"She can't be that bad." I finished my coffee, feeling better already.

"She wanted Gran to paint the café to match her art gallery."

I laughed. "I can't see that happening." Gran's Café was firmly ensconced in its original mid-twentieth-century diner decor, inside and out.

"Yeah. Neither could Gran. They had words over it. Gran kicked her out of the café."

"Gran? But she gets along with everyone."

"Not Caro Lewis. I hope the two of them can ignore each other for the summer."

I put my empty coffee cup in the dishwasher. "It's time to start the coffee for the guests."

"We have eight for breakfast this morning?"

"Yes. There's a family from Pennsylvania checking in this afternoon and another couple from Minnesota, so tomorrow morning there will be a full house."

Becky opened her laptop and started making notes. "Does the family have young children?"

"I don't think so. Mrs. Thomas asked about our wi-fi for her daughters."

"Too bad. I found some great kid-friendly breakfast recipes I'm anxious to try."

"One of the reservations for the middle of June asked about a crib."

Becky did a fist pump. "Yes! Little kids! They're the best."

"Let's take care of this week's guests first. It's past time for me to get to work."

By the time I had the coffee brewing in the dining room, Rose had come out of her suite with Thatcher running ahead of her.

"Good morning." I scratched the corgi's ears while Rose shrugged her jacket on. "How's my favorite pup this morning?"

"Ready to roll." Rose gave me a good morning hug. "And you?" She backed away and frowned as she looked at me. "You look a little tired."

I gave my aunt a gentle push toward the door. "I stayed up too late last night."

"Reading again?" She stopped at the door and turned toward me with a smile. "I'm the same way." She gave me a conspiratorial wink and took Thatcher out for their morning walk.

Just as she left, Violet and Charles Bishop came out of the Summerwine suite, located off the dining room.

"Good morning." I greeted the elderly couple with a smile. "Breakfast won't be ready until seven o'clock, but coffee and tea are available."

Viperish Violet. I regretted the mnemonic that had

popped into my head when they had checked in the afternoon before, but Violet's long, thin body coiled in her wheelchair reminded me of a snake. I would have to come up with a different mnemonic to erase my first impression. Her husband was the opposite. When they had visited with Rose the evening before, he had said he was a retired pharmacist. With his kind and caring manner, I could imagine he had been a favorite with his customers.

Charitable Charles gave me a smile. "We thought we would take our tea on the veranda this morning. Would that be too much trouble?"

"Not at all. You can choose your favorite blend and I'll help you get settled. The deck next to the library is in the sunshine this time of the morning. How does that sound?"

"It would be lovely," Violet said.

I had gotten Violet and Charles settled on the sunny, sheltered deck and was refilling the cream pitcher at the coffee station when I heard a door slam on the second floor. Betty Ann and Sally Marie Brooks were on their way down the stairs. The senior sisters from South Carolina were staying in the Dublin Bay. I didn't need to use mnemonics to remember their names.

"It's too early for breakfast, isn't it?" That was Sally Marie, the older one.

"Look at my watch. It's nearly eight-thirty. Breakfast has been ready for more than an hour."

They clumped down the stairs. Both sisters had donned hiking boots as soon as they had reached the Black Hills, but I doubted they would do much hiking during their stay. Their flowing blouses over bright capris were a cacophony of color that reminded me of a swirl of butterflies in a flower garden. Large, showy butterflies.

Betty Ann spied me as soon as they reached the bottom of the stairs.

"There's Emma! Yoo-hoo!" Her voice rose even higher in volume. "We aren't too late for breakfast, are we?"

I met them before they reached the reception desk. "It's only six-thirty, ladies. Please keep your voices down. The other guests are still sleeping."

"Six-thirty?" Betty Ann's voice was as loud as ever. "How can it be six-thirty? Look at my watch." She held her arm up to my face.

"We talked about this yesterday, remember? The Black Hills are in the Mountain Time Zone. Your watch is still set for Eastern Time."

"Oh, my, she's right," Sally Marie said, turning to her sister. "We forgot again."

"There is tea or coffee if you would like some. You could sit on the front porch and enjoy the morning while you wait for breakfast."

Betty Ann pushed past me, pointing out the French doors on the other side of the dining room. "Look, Sally Marie. I told you I saw a woman in a wheelchair when we came in last night, and there she is."

I was glad the Bishops were on the other side of the closed doors, but I hadn't reckoned with the sisters' determination. In spite of my maneuvering, they slipped past me through the dining room, and out the doors to the deck.

"Good morning," Betty Ann said, sticking her hand out to the couple. "I'm Betty Ann and that's Sally Marie. We're the Brooks sisters."

Sally Marie took Violet's hand and shook it vigorously. "Everyone thinks we're twins, but we're not. Mama and Daddy loved me so much when I was born that they had Betty Ann right away. She's always been my baby doll."

Betty Ann picked up the thread even before Sally Marie dropped it. "We're from Oxford Springs, South Carolina. If there's anything we can do for y'all, just let us know. We love to help those who are less fortunate. Mama always said it was why God put us on this good earth."

Violet withdrew her hand from Sally Marie's grasp, her face red. I tried to detour the sisters.

"Let's get your coffee, ladies, or would you rather have tea this morning? Didn't you want to sit on the front porch? We still have a half hour before breakfast is ready."

It worked.

"We'll have coffee," Sally Marie said, turning back toward the dining room. "Come on, Betty Ann. You can put in as much of the pink sweetener as you like."

Betty Ann followed her. "Oh, my," she said. "Look at my watch. Is it really eight-thirty?"

"We've been through that, dear. You need to reset your watch."

As the ladies went to the coffee maker, I closed the French doors. Violet's expression was stony, but when Charles leaned over and asked her something, she shook her head and waved him away. Her face relaxed as she picked up her cup with a shaking hand. Charles reached over to steady the cup for her, and she gave him a smile of gratitude. They seemed to have forgiven the intrusion.

I left them and went to help the sisters get settled

on the porch. I had my work cut out for me during their stay.

At seven o'clock, Dave and Joy Albert, a retired couple from Michigan, came downstairs.

"You're right on time," I said. "Breakfast is on the buffet."

"It smells delicious," Joy said. "Are we the first ones up?"

"The others will be in soon, I'm sure. The Bishops are on the library deck, and the Brooks sisters from South Carolina are on the front porch. I'm on my way to let them know breakfast is ready now."

Joy beamed. "I love those two ladies! I grew up in South Carolina, and their accents bring back so many memories."

As Dave and Joy went on into the dining room, I continued to the front porch. Rose and Thatcher had returned from their walk and my aunt was chatting with the ladies.

Betty Ann was holding Thatcher on her lap. "Isn't he the most darling little dog?"

Thatcher looked at me and grinned, his eyes half closed. He was enjoying the attention.

Betty Ann continued. "I told Sally Marie we should get a dog like this sweetie, but she said no." Her face dropped into a pout for a second before resuming her normal happy expression.

"Our building doesn't allow dogs, remember?" Sally Marie patted her sister's arm. "But you can enjoy him while we're here."

"I'll take Thatcher in," Rose said, lifting him off Betty Ann's lap and setting him on the porch. "It's time for breakfast."

Sally Marie stood and tugged Betty Ann to her feet. "Breakfast is the best part of staying at a B&B, isn't it?"

"I know you'll enjoy Becky's baked omelet this morning." I opened the door for the ladies as they walked through and into the dining room.

Rose paused at the door before she and Thatcher went inside. "How are the other guests this morning?"

"All in a good mood. Joy Albert was hoping to spend some time talking to the Brooks sisters."

"That's good. I like to see the guests enjoying themselves."

I do, too, I thought as I went into the dining room. The Alberts were sharing a table with Betty Ann and Sally Marie.

"It's good to meet someone from home," Joy said. "Even after living in Detroit for thirty years, South Carolina is in my blood."

"And always will be," Sally Marie said. "Home is home, no matter where we roam."

"We visit every year," Dave said. "Spring break at the beach while the kids were growing up, and now that we're retired, we spend a few weeks there every winter."

The French doors by the library opened and Charles wheeled Violet to their suite. He parked her wheelchair outside the door, then came over to me. He cleared his throat.

"We hate to impose, but sometimes my wife is uncomfortable eating in front of other people. She's having a difficult time this morning."

I remembered her shaking hand as she lifted her

teacup earlier.

"I understand. Would you like to have your breakfast in your suite?"

"If you don't mind."

"It isn't a problem at all. I'll get a tray."

Charles filled two plates while I readied a teapot and added a saucer with extra tea and sweetener to the tray. I carried it to their suite and set it on the counter in their kitchenette. Then I helped Charles clear the small table. There were several artistic photographs in frames that he stacked together and took into the living area.

"Gifts for our nieces," Violet said. "We found them at a cute little shop in the town yesterday."

"I'm sure they'll appreciate them," I said, and left the couple to their breakfasts.

Once our morning work was completed, Becky and I walked down Graves' Gulch Road to Gran's Café in Paragon. Even though the inn was officially part of the small town, our location on the opposite side of the highway from the rest of the homes and businesses kept us separate. But Becky's family consisting of Gran, sisters, brothers, and assorted aunts, uncles, and cousins had made Rose and I feel welcome.

"There sure are a lot more people around than last week," I said as we waited for three cars to go by before crossing the road.

"The tourist season has officially started." Becky waved to a young man I hadn't seen before. "Memorial Day weekend is the big kickoff, and we'll see crowds until the middle of August, when schools start again."

"Who did you wave to?"

"That's Jack Pike. He and his wife Shasta own Come on Up where they sell hiking and climbing gear."

"Their store must be one that's closed during the winter."

"Yup. He and Shasta head to New Mexico during the winter months. They have another store there."

"Do many of the shopkeepers do the same?"

"Most of them." Becky paused at the door of Gran's Café and pointed west down Main Street, away from the center of town. "Old Stumpy, Gran's brother-in-law, is one of the year-'rounders. He spends the off-season hunting for antlers and bones in the forest and preparing his merchandise. All of it is local. He opens up his shop in April."

"He sells antlers?"

"Lots of stuff. People use animal bones, sinew, teeth, and antlers to make traditional jewelry and decorations. He also sells supplies for bead work."

"I can't believe those things are popular enough to support a store."

Becky grinned. "Remember, you're in South Dakota. A lot of Lakota do traditional crafts like bead work. Gran makes beautiful beaded moccasins for the dancers."

I shook my head. "You've lost me. Dancers?"

"Girl, you're coming with me to the next Powwow. You'll be blown away." She opened the screen door and pushed me into the café. "I'm starving. Let's get some lunch."

Cheeseburgers and fries were on the menu. I tried not to indulge more than once a week, but Gran's burgers were the perfect balance of tasty and decadently juicy. I opted for sweet potato fries, and

Becky made sure there was a dill pickle spear on my plate.

Thirty minutes later, I was ready to walk off my lunch. We headed out to Main Street.

"We'll start on this side, then cross the street down at Cloud Creek Road and come back on the other side."

"Are all of the businesses here on Main Street?"

"Yup. Great-grandpa Graves laid out the town in nineteen-thirty. He plotted out Main Street and Church Street with both running parallel to the highway.

The highway was one of the routes between Rapid City and Mount Rushmore and hugged the base of Grizzly Peak as it climbed into the Hills. Main Street followed that same curve.

"Then in around nineteen-fifty, his son added the side streets and named them after his granddaughters. Willow is behind us, then Maggie. You know her as Gran. Then Sadie and Jeanne." Becky pointed down the street. "Each one of the side streets is one block long, so it's a simple plan. The stores are here on Main, and the houses are along Church Street. Mackenzie's Draw Road is on the west end of town and heads up into the Hills."

"Where does it go?"

"If you follow it far enough, you'll get to Hill City. But you'd want four-wheel-drive to take that one out of town."

We walked past the ice cream shop next to the café. The line of customers wound down the sidewalk, and Becky waved to the girls behind the counter.

"The sign says Gran's Ice Cream. I didn't know

she had two stores," I said.

"The ice cream shop is only open in the summer. The high school kids staff it, and they work hard. It's big bragging rights if Gran chooses you to work there."

"Don't tell me. You worked there in high school."

"I was the manager two years in a row," Becky said and gave me a high-five. "Let's stop here."

We pushed open the door of a bookstore. I took a deep breath as a bell tinkled over our heads. Bookstores were the nicest smelling places in the world, and in this one the heavenly fragrance of coffee mingled with the books.

"Hi, Ashley," Becky said as a woman about our age walked toward us. Her light brown hair was caught up in a ponytail.

Ashley pushed up her glasses. "Hi, Becky." She held out her hand to me. "You must be Emma. Becky told me how you caught a murderer last month. That must have been exciting."

Her smile was inviting me to divulge all the details of a time I would rather forget. I understood when I saw the book in her hand with her finger as a bookmark. It was the latest mystery to hit the best sellers list. I grinned back at her as I shook her hand.

"Catching a killer in real life isn't the same as in a book or on television. I'm just happy it's over."

Ashley looked a little disappointed. "No more murders? I was hoping there would be a sequel."

I laughed. "I hope not." I held up one of my brochures. "I wondered if you would have room on your counter to put a few of these out. We would be happy to recommend your store to our guests in exchange."

"That's a great idea," she said. She took the brochure and used it as a marker in her book, then went over to the sales counter. "I got in some bookmarks advertising Between the Pages. Would you be able to make them available to your guests?"

"Sure." I exchanged a stack of brochures for the bookmarks and put them in my bag. "What kinds of books do you sell?"

"Almost every genre, both new and used. I buy and sell online, too. The store's website is on the bookmark."

"Gran told me you're planning to be a permanent resident," Becky said.

"That's right."

"You mean you won't be one of the businesses that moves south for the winter?" I asked.

Ashley shook her head. "That kind of life isn't for me. I want to put my roots down, and Paragon is the place to do it, even though my last name isn't Graves." She winked at Becky.

"They let a few of us outsiders in," I said. "Although I don't think there's a danger of the Graves family being outnumbered."

"I'm looking forward to getting to know both of you," Ashley said as we made our way to the door. "We should have lunch sometime."

"Will you have time for lunch?" I glanced at the hours posted on her door. Between the Pages was open from nine until eight daily.

She sighed. "Probably not until the end of the season."

"I have an idea," said Becky. "We'll get lunch from Gran's sometime and bring it over. We can eat and visit between customers."

"I'd like that," Ashley said.

She picked up her book again as I followed Becky out to the sidewalk. I reached into my bag to pull out another stack of brochures and ran right into a khaki shirt.

"Whoa, Emma. Watch where you're going."

Strong hands grabbed my arms and steadied me when I nearly fell backward.

Cowboy Cal. I told my stomach to settle down.

"Hey, Cal," Becky said. "What are you doing?"

His eyes hadn't left mine. I hadn't seen much of Becky's cousin since he had arrested Wil last month. Becky said he had gone out of town for a week of training somewhere, but that didn't explain where he had been for the other three weeks. Or why he hadn't called me. Or why he hadn't followed up after we had to cancel the date-that-wasn't-a-date.

"I'm heading to the café for lunch. What are you up to?"

I handed one of the brochures to him. "Spreading these around town. I want to advertise the inn a little and pick up some literature from the shops for our guests at the same time."

Raised voices from across the street drew our attention. The shorter woman raised her hand, threatening to hit the taller one with a... rolling pin?

"Not again," Cal said as he started across the street to the two women arguing in front of the art gallery.

"Again?" I said, jogging next to him. Becky was right behind me.

He didn't answer me but stepped between the two ladies.

"Ms. Sminski, give me the rolling pin."

He took it out of her hand, but she didn't look at

him. Ms. Sminski was a short woman with bleached blond curls wearing a t-shirt and jeans. The woman facing her was tall, thin, and dressed to kill in a black and white pantsuit.

"You arrest her, you policeman," Ms. Sminski yelled. I recognized her accent from one of the Slavic countries. "She wants to take my store. Make it into what? A studio?"

The other woman sniffed. "I only made the suggestion."

"Suggestion with teeth. You said you would burn store down!"

"Ms. Lewis," Cal said, his voice even. "Did you threaten to burn down her store?"

The other woman seemed to grow even taller. "I did not. I only said it should be burned. She has the temerity to call her merchandise art." She waved her hand toward the other side of the street. "She sells junk. It's all imported junk."

"Olga, you need to go back to your store," Cal said. "And in the future, come to me if you have a complaint to make against someone."

Olga Sminski's eyes shifted away from Cal. "I do not call policeman. No good comes from calling police."

"This isn't Slovakia," Cal said. "I'm here to help."

She took her rolling pin back and scuttled across Main Street. He turned toward Ms. Lewis, but she had already disappeared inside the art gallery.

"There we go," he said. "Just another summer day in Paragon."

Two

Cal brushed some dust off his shirt sleeve. "Those women are like two mountain lions fighting for territory."

"Who are they?" I asked.

He gestured toward the art gallery. "That one is Caro Lewis. You've heard about her art gallery?"

I nodded. "Becky told me a little bit about it."

"The other one is Olga Sminski. She and her brother Simon own a couple tourist traps on Main Street. She sells souvenirs and Simon sells t-shirts. They were here last year, too. Nice folks if you don't get in their way."

"She didn't seem to trust you."

"Yup." Cal rubbed his chin as he watched Olga enter her shop across the street. "Makes me wonder why." He turned back to us. "I had better get to Gran's for my lunch. It's been great seeing you again, Emma."

"Maybe we can do it again sometime." I watched him make his way toward the café until I lost him in the crowd in front of the ice cream shop, then I turned to Becky. "What is it with him? He didn't act like he was glad to see me or anything."

"I have no idea. He's always been a little shy with girls. Maybe you intimidate him."

"Me? Intimidating?" I laughed.

"Yeah." Becky linked her arm in mine and started across the street toward the Grizzly Peak Grill. "You're smart, pretty, you dress nicely, and people like you. Cal might think you're out of his league, dating-wise."

"What can I do to change his opinion?"

"Whatever you do, don't change yourself. He likes you. Just be his friend."

The Grizzly Peak Grill, next to Olga's souvenir shop, was set back from the street. Along the sidewalk was a covered patio with several tables. Three sets of doors were open between the restaurant and the patio, giving passers-by a glimpse inside, the shadowed room a cool contrast to the sunny seating in front. As we approached, Violet and Charles came out the center door and turned in the opposite direction.

Becky started to wave, but they hadn't seen us. "Isn't that-"

"Yes. Violet and Charles. We don't need to interrupt their outing. We'll see them at the inn this afternoon for tea."

"Tea!" Becky clapped her hand over her mouth. "I can't believe I forgot to make the scones for this afternoon's tea, and new guests will be checking in." She thrust the bag with her share of the brochures into my hand. "I'm sorry, but you'll have to do the rest of these on your own. I've got to get back to the inn."

Then she was gone, leaving me alone on the sidewalk. I slung Becky's tote bag over my shoulder as

I walked into the restaurant.

"Is your manager available?" I asked the girl at the hostess stand. She couldn't have been more than fourteen years old.

She gave me a practiced smile. "I can help you."

I held out one of the brochures. "I'm Emma Blackwood from the Sweetbrier Inn. Is there a place where you could make these available to your customers?"

Her face fell. "Um. I'll get my dad."

While I waited, I looked around the restaurant. It was after one o'clock but most of the tables were full. The atmosphere was casual, and the aroma tickled my appetite, even though I had just finished lunch. This was a place I would have to come back to sometime. Maybe if Cal and I ever rescheduled the date-that-wasn't-a-date.

A forty-something man wearing an apron came from the kitchen, following the hostess.

"Nicole said you wanted to see me. I'm Matthew Brannon, owner of the Grizzly Peak Grill."

I handed him a brochure and repeated my introduction. "Would it be all right if I left a few of these here for your customers? I'd be happy to return the favor."

His face was thoughtful as he looked through the brochure. "That would be great. We have some to-go menus you could make available for your guests." He led me farther into the restaurant to the cashier's stand and handed me some fliers with the menu and the restaurant's logo. "I'm curious, though. I had gotten the feeling the merchants in Paragon weren't interested in cooperating with each other."

I thought of the altercation between Olga and

Caro. "I hope not. It's in our best interests to work together, isn't it?"

He leaned on the counter. "I think so, but Caro Lewis stopped by yesterday for lunch. When I suggested the possibility of catering a wine tasting at her art gallery, she turned me down flat."

"Maybe she doesn't like wine?"

He grinned, his smile a natural copy of his daughter's. "I doubt it. Not the way she was enjoying the bottle she ordered with her lunch."

"Is she the only one in town who doesn't want to cooperate?"

"Have you met my neighbor?" He thumbed in the direction of Olga Sminski's souvenir shop. "She and her brother are both only interested in their stores' sales, not getting chummy with the neighbors. And they aren't the only ones. The only other person who will talk to me is Ashley from the bookstore. Everyone else seems to be too busy. How can we form a welcoming community if we won't talk to each other?"

"Maybe we can change that." I placed a stack of brochures on the counter and put his fliers in my bag. "With you, Ashley, and the Sweetbrier Inn, there are at least a few of us who will work together, right?"

"It's a start." He shook my hand. "It was great to meet you, Emma."

Mellow Matthew and his daughter Nervous Nicole. I repeated the mnemonics in my head so I would remember them. How many other friendly faces would I find along the way?

I continued down Main, stopping at the t-shirt store run by Olga's brother, Simon. I wasn't surprised when he turned me down.

When I reached the last business on the east end of the street I looked up at the sign.

"Hogs and Suds?"

A man wiping off tables on the front patio grinned at me. His stained apron covered a generous belly.

"Hogs and Suds. Get it?" My face must have shown my confusion. "Hogs, as in bikes." His explanation didn't clear up anything. "Harleys. Bikers call them hogs."

"Okay. But what about the suds? Is this a laundromat?"

He laughed. "Suds. You know. The head of foam on a beer."

A woman dressed in jeans and a black leather vest came out of the building and joined him. "It's a play on the old drive in, Dog and Suds. Get it?"

I laughed. "Now I do. You cater to motorcycle riders?"

They both beamed. "We're the best biker bar in the Hills, outside of Sturgis," the man said. "We really get swinging when the bikers show up."

The woman elbowed her husband. "I'm Barb and this is Billy."

I introduced myself and my errand. "I'd be happy to advertise your business at the inn."

Billy frowned. "You must not be part of Caro's crowd."

"Caro Lewis?"

He nodded his head in the direction of the town's center. "Her and her big city ways. Comes in here and tells us our bar doesn't belong in Paragon."

"Why would she do that?"

Barb sniffed. "We're not good enough for her. She said she had a vision to turn Paragon into a haven for the arts." Her voice turned into a growl. "I'd like to haven her."

Billy leaned closer. "We've been here more than twenty years. Who does she think she is to try to kick us out?"

"She's new in town, isn't she?"

"We ran into her when we opened for the season last month," Barb said. "We spend the winters in Texas, then have this place open from the end of April until October. You must have seen her purple and pink monstrosity. Not exactly Paragon's style."

"I don't know where she got her idea the town would go along with this place becoming an art colony." Billy went back to clearing tables. "That isn't Paragon's scene, you know?"

The art colony idea was interesting, but in Paragon? A place like Hogs and Suds would definitely be unwelcome in the kind of atmosphere an art colony desired.

"Is she the only one pushing for this?"

Barb shrugged. "We have no idea. When she talked about the art colony, it sounded like she had some kind of committee backing her up. But the other merchants are either mad at Caro or intimidated by her. Except for Maggie Graves. That lady is tough and doesn't back down for anyone."

I had to agree with Barb about her assessment of Gran.

"How does Caro intimidate people?"

"It isn't what she does as much as it's her attitude. She assumes people are going to go along with her, and before you know it you find yourself agreeing with everything she's saying until, BAM, you've painted yourself into a corner." Barb's face grew red.

"She's sneaky."

"Now don't get upset about that all over again." Billy put an arm around his wife. "Caro had Barb agreeing we needed more art galleries and studios in town, and before she knew it, Caro was making suggestions of how to turn our biker bar into an art studio. She said we could start a new bar closer to Sturgis."

Barb nodded. "All she wants to do is shut us down. She can have her art gallery - it's no skin off my nose - but when she tries to drive us away..." She balled her fists. "It makes me mad all over again."

I said goodbye to Biker Billy and Bristly Barb and crossed Main Street to the combination convenience store and gas station. From there I made my way back down the other side of Main, stopping at every business. At all of them, the fudge and taffy shop, the deli, a cute gift shop called Living Wild, and the sports store, I found the same attitude. Most were willing to place my brochures in their shops, but no one had anything good to say about the owner of the art gallery.

When I left Jack, the owner of Come on Up, I saw the art gallery ahead of me. Adjoining it was an old-time photo place and my last stop.

I was on the corner of Maggie Street and Main, across from the ice cream stand. I paused to gather my forces before facing Caro Lewis. Over the past month, the wood-frame building had been remodeled into a funky, artistic style I had seen in other towns that attracted tourists who were interested in art. The turquoise and fuchsia swirl patterns competed with purple and pink blocks, highlighting the artsy feeling. And the whimsical lettering was cute. It added a fun touch of shabby chic to the town. Caro Lewis might do well with her gallery, but I wasn't sure she would ever convince the rest of the town to go along with the transformation into an art colony.

Grabbing a handful of brochures out of my bag, I pushed open the door of the gallery. Art pieces were placed around the room, most with a Native American theme. Bold paintings, unique photographs, and collections of sculptures filled the large open room. It looked like several artists were represented.

On the wall behind a counter was a large modern painting. Splashes of color in cool tones of lavender and blue filled the background, overlaid with swashes of green. I stepped closer. There was a signature in the corner of the painting, and I walked around the counter to examine it.

That's when something gave away under my shoe. I jumped back. Then I saw her.

Caro Lewis was lying on the floor behind the counter, her eyes staring and empty.

I knelt next to her to check for a pulse.

Nothing. Her wrist was still warm to the touch, but there was no life in her.

I grabbed my phone and scrolled to Cal's number.

When Cal answered his phone, I could tell he was still at Gran's Café from the background noises.

"Hey Emma, what's up?"

"I'm going to need your help."

"To pass out the brochures?"

I walked over to the window where I had a view of Gran's.

"No. I've run into a problem at Caro Lewis' art

gallery."

"Did she get into another argument with someone?"

I glanced behind me at the still form behind the counter. "She won't be arguing with anyone again. She's dead."

Three seconds later, Cal charged out of the café door and headed across the street at a jog. I opened the door for him, then turned the sign to 'closed' as I shut it and turned the deadbolt.

"Where is she?"

"Behind the counter."

Cal circled the end of the counter. I followed until he stopped and held out an arm to keep me from coming too close.

"Careful. We don't want to contaminate the crime scene."

"I think I already did." I pointed to the brochures that had fallen out of my hand and onto the body when I had stepped on her. "Are you sure it's a crime scene?"

"It's an unattended death, so it's a potential crime scene."

"Uh huh." I crossed my arms. "Or is it only a crime scene because I'm the one who found her?"

"You are getting a reputation." Cal gave me a sideways look as he handed me a pair of gloves, then turned back to his investigation.

While Cal examined Caro, I took a second look. The body was sprawled on the floor as if she had fainted. A framed picture was next to her, face down. It looked like she had been holding it when she fell.

"Could she have had a heart attack, or a stroke?" I asked.

"That's a possibility. There isn't any sign of foul play. No blood or bullet holes. No sign of a head injury. At least we know the approximate time of death."

"Right. We both saw her arguing with Olga on the sidewalk an hour ago."

"I need to get my bag from my vehicle." He started to the door, then turned back to me. "I hope I don't need to remind you not to touch anything."

I crossed my arms over my stomach and shivered. "No problem."

While Cal was gone, I went back to the painting on the wall behind the counter, careful to avoid Caro's body. The signature was Caro's, and a plaque next to it identified it as *Almost Spring* by Caro Lewis. Another line said it had won an award given by a museum in Chicago in nineteen-seventy-three. On the left side of the display was a small sign indicating the painting was not for sale.

I walked around the gallery. The large area was divided by hanging fabric panels into spaces highlighting a different artist in each. One space had small paintings of scenery from South Dakota. I recognized the Badlands and Black Elk Peak in the Black Hills. Another space had several small sculptures of motorcycles, all made from rusty nuts and bolts. The next space was larger, and featured Papier Mâché sculptures. I looked closely at one of a horse that was caught in mid-stride. I could almost feel the wind blowing through its mane and tail.

Even though the displays were well organized and the artwork was attractive, there were no other pieces as impressive as Caro's painting.

Cal returned with his duffel bag and knelt next to

the body. I knew what was coming next as he fulfilled his duty as assistant coroner, and I didn't want to be around for that part of the investigation. I went into the back room.

I wasn't sure what I would find back there, but I didn't expect cardboard boxes. I pulled the flap open on one sitting on a table. It was filled with flat wrapped objects, most of them about a foot square. I checked the return address on the box. China? The other six boxes had the same label. Had Caro been importing art for her gallery from China?

Next to the table was a personal refrigerator, the kind college students have in their dorm rooms. Inside were bottles of probiotic drinks and a couple containers of sliced fruits and veggies. On top of the fridge was a box of protein bars.

I picked up a brochure from a stack on the table. It advertised the art gallery and boasted of art from local artists. An entire page highlighted Lakota artists.

"Hey, Cal." I went back up front. "You've got to see this. There are shipping boxes from China back there."

He stripped off his latex gloves. "That's not illegal."

"But according to this brochure, she represented local artists in her gallery."

"Still not illegal, even if it might be deceptive." He packed his gear back into the duffel bag and stood up. "It looks like you're right about the heart attack. It seems to be the most likely cause of death."

I took another look at Caro. She looked fit, and from the snacks I saw in the back, she seemed to be pretty health conscious.

"She doesn't look like the heart attack type," I

said.

"What do you mean?"

"Look at her. She isn't carrying any extra weight, her muscles look toned, and from the looks of the fridge in the back, she wasn't addicted to junk food."

"That doesn't mean she didn't have a heart attack."

"No, but it makes it less likely."

He chewed on his toothpick. "Are you trying to say there's something suspicious about her death?"

"Maybe. Something doesn't seem right."

Cal pulled his phone from his belt. "I need to call this in. We'll see what the coroner says once she gets to the morgue. Then you can show me what you found in the back."

Cal pulled on a fresh pair of latex gloves as we walked into the back room. Cal peered into the box on the table. He pulled out one of the flat objects and handed it to me while he started unwrapping a second one.

"It's a picture," I said as I pulled away the thin foam sheeting. "It looks like it is Native American art, but from China?"

"This one, too." Cal held his up and compared it to mine. "They're cheap knockoffs. The kind you'd find in a souvenir shop."

"Someone killed Caro because they were angry when they found out she had sold them a fake?"

Cal stared at me. "You think someone killed Caro over souvenir art?" He turned to another box and slit it open with his knife. "And how did he do that? He frightened her to death?"

"Okay. Maybe that theory doesn't work."

"Your theory assumes Caro was murdered. We

have no evidence to indicate that."

"Not yet." I peered into the box Cal had opened. More wrapped pictures. "Does she have any authentic art in the gallery?"

Cal walked back into the front of the store while I followed. He stopped at the display of metal motorcycles. "I recognize this guy's name." He pointed to the next booth with the Papier Mâché horse I had admired. "And these pieces are authentic. The artist lives here in Paragon."

"He's a cousin?"

Cal actually smiled. "She's my second cousin, Amelia."

I looked at her other pieces. One was of a mother with a child and others were of coyotes in different poses and other animals. The sculptures were about eighteen inches high, and perfect for someone to display in their office or home. I wasn't surprised at the high prices.

"What is going on here? Is this a high-end art gallery, or a cheap souvenir shop?" I pointed at the next display of the same style pictures as we had found in the back room. "There are the cheap knockoffs." I picked one up and examined it. "And no label saying they're from China."

"And these prices are in the same range as the originals. It looks like this is where she was making her money."

"Isn't that illegal? Misrepresenting what she's selling?"

Cal pointed to the sign identifying the display. "Look at the artist's name."

"Caro Lewis?" I looked back at the painting on the wall behind the sales counter. "They don't look anything like that painting on display. Completely different style."

"Something is fishy here," Cal said, "but not illegal as far as I can tell. These could be prints of her original art she had made in China. I'll have to look into it further."

"We have another murder investigation?" The queasy feeling in my stomach had nothing to do with the handsome deputy standing next to me.

He frowned. "First of all, we have no evidence there has been a murder. And second? There is no 'we.' Let the police handle this one, Emma." He shifted the toothpick to the opposite corner of his mouth. "And you can't tell anyone about this. We need to notify her family before anyone else hears about her death."

As Cal ushered me toward the door, I took a last glance at Caro's body. He was probably right that she died of natural causes, but I couldn't shake the feeling there was something hinky about this whole situation.

Three

I was glad the old-time photo shop had been closed when I passed by because I'm not sure how I would have faced another shop owner after what I had just experienced. Finding a dead body might be something I had done more than most people in the past month, but that didn't mean I liked it.

As I walked up Graves' Gulch Road toward the inn, I had another sinking thought. Cal had told me not to tell anyone about Caro's death for now, but did he mean I had to keep it a secret from Rose and Becky, too? With one look at my face, they would both know something had happened. I would make a terrible poker player.

Five minutes before three. I walked in the door right on time.

I stashed the remainder of the brochures under the reception desk and took out the fliers I had picked up from the businesses in Paragon. For now, I arranged them on the end of the desk where we kept brochures and menus from other businesses in Rapid City and around the Black Hills. I made a mental note to find a better spot for them. Perhaps a display rack that would stand right inside the front door.

Walking into the dining room, I waved to Becky through the pass-through window at the buffet counter.

"Hey, girl," she said. "Did you get to the rest of the stores in town?"

"No problem."

She had been placing scones on the serving plate but stopped and pierced my flippant answer with a look. "You're sure there was no problem?"

I couldn't meet her eyes. "Yeah. I met some great people, too. Do you know Billy and Barb?"

She covered the serving plate with plastic wrap to keep the scones fresh until our four o'clock tea.

"The Barkers? Barb is my mom's cousin. They're family."

I started a fresh pot of coffee and checked the supply of tea bags.

"What happened, Emma? There's something you're not telling me."

"Nothing." I refilled the basket of sugar packets and other sweeteners.

"You're a terrible liar." Becky leaned on the counter between us. "Did you have a run-in with Cal? Did he blow you off again? If he did, I'll talk some sense into him."

"I saw Cal, but he was fine. Back to his old self."

Becky's mouth made an O. "That means he has a case! What happened? Was one of the stores robbed?"

I faced her over the counter. "How do you do that? I didn't tell you anything."

"I know my cousin. If he's in a good mood, it's because he has something to investigate. I'll bet he told you not to say anything to me, didn't he?"

"Okay. Yes. Something happened and I can't tell you."

"What are you girls talking about?"

I hadn't heard Rose come out of her suite. She joined us at the counter as she made herself a cup of tea.

"Cal said I needed to keep it quiet."

Becky grinned. "He didn't mean us. We're part of the team, right? If there's something to investigate, we're on it."

This had to stop. Any minute now someone would walk in on our conversation and then everyone would know.

"Okay. You win. But I promised Cal I wouldn't tell anyone about this, so it has to stay between the three of us."

They waited while I took a deep breath.

"Caro Lewis is dead."

"You're kidding, right?" Becky asked. "Another murder?"

"It looks like she probably had a heart attack, but Cal is waiting until he gets the results of the autopsy."

Rose stirred some honey into her tea. "That poor woman. I met her a few times."

"What did you think of her?" I asked.

"She was...difficult." Rose paused as she laid her teaspoon on a napkin. "She assumed we had a lot in common, since we were both single businesswomen on the far side of fifty. I had to tell her my interests in art were broad but don't include modern art, and she took offense. She had a manner that didn't invite friendship."

"I got the same feeling from the other

businesspeople in town. That's what makes me wonder if her death wasn't from natural causes."

"You mean you think she rubbed someone the wrong way and they killed her for it?" Becky nodded her head as she spoke. "Because I could totally see that happening."

"Not me." I glanced at Rose for confirmation. "People don't normally get killed only because someone doesn't like them. There needs to be a deeper reason."

"Emma is right," Rose said. "Caro may have been overbearing and abrasive, but that isn't a motive for murder. Her death was most likely from natural causes and Cal is going by the book."

The front door opened, and I turned to greet our new guests. Dad, mom, two girls. This had to be the Thomas family. I slipped behind the reception desk.

"Good afternoon," I said, opening the guest registration book. "I'm Emma Blackwood. Welcome to Rose's Sweetbrier Inn."

"Hi." The mom, a professional looking African American woman, guided the younger daughter in front of her as she approached the desk. The girl's attention was on her tablet and the game she was playing. "We have reservations. Terri Thomas. This is my husband, Ted." He nodded in my direction, then went back to perusing the brochures. "And our daughters, Taylor and Toni."

She gave Toni a nudge, but the girl didn't look up. Taylor was staring at her phone but gave me a little wave when her mom said her name. She looked like she was about fourteen, while Toni was still in the kid stage at ten years old or so.

"It's nice to meet you," I said as I turned the guest

register toward her. "We have you in the Snow Goose and Albertine rooms. They connect to make a two-bedroom suite."

Terri paused with her pen hovering over the page. "I don't think I've ever signed a guest register before. You people are pretty old-school, aren't you?"

I laughed. "Rose like things to be simple."

"But your website was so up to date. I though the inn would be, too." She looked like she was having second thoughts.

"Don't worry. The inn is very modern, with every convenience you might wish for. But at the same time, we encourage our guests to relax and enjoy their stay away from their regular routines."

Ted came up behind his wife and put an arm around her shoulders. "Remember why we came here? Like Emma said, it's time to relax and spend some family time together."

Terri smiled at me. "Ted is right. We chose this place because it was as far away from the city as we could get without going too rustic. We wanted to give our girls a place where they could unplug."

"Unplug?" Taylor's anguished voice made us all look at her. "You said I could use my phone."

"Remember the deal?" Ted asked. "You get two hours a day. The rest of the time your mom or I hold on to the electronics."

Toni looked up. "You mean you were serious about that?"

"Very." Terri finished signing the guest register and handed me her credit card. "We'll start in the morning. You decide when you use your two hours, but when they're done, so is the screen time until the next morning."

Taylor groaned, but Toni turned back to her game with renewed vigor. "Then I'm going to finish this level before you take it away."

"I'll help you take your luggage up to your room so you can settle in," I said as I came to the front of the desk. "We serve tea at four o'clock every afternoon, and breakfast is from seven until nine o'clock." I started up the stairs with one of the suitcases. "There are places to hike, and some fun shops in the town, as well as the many attractions in the area. If you have any questions, we'll be glad to help you find your way around."

Taylor caught up with me at the top of the staircase. "Did I see a library downstairs?"

"Yes. It's on the other side of the dining room, past the piano."

"Are we allowed to read the books?"

A girl after my own heart. "Of course, you are. Books are meant to be read. Please let one of us know if you want to remove a book from the inn, though." I extended the handle on the wheeled suitcase and walked beside Taylor through the upstairs lounge to their rooms. "Is there a particular author you like?"

"I'm reading through Agatha Christie's books this summer, but my books are on my phone, and you heard what Mom and Dad just said."

"Then you'll love the library. Rose has the entire collection of Christie's works."

Terri had overheard us. "An entire collection? That's impressive."

I smiled at both of them as I unlocked the door of the Snow Goose. "You'll have to ask Rose about them. We're both big fans of Agatha Christie's stories."

Setting the suitcase in the Snow Goose, I handed the keys to Terri, then opened the pass-through door between the two rooms. "I'll leave you to get settled in."

Back behind the reception desk, I greeted Violet and Charles as they came in the front door.

"Did you have a good time in town?"

Violet frowned, peering at me. "How did you know we were in town?"

"I was there, too, and saw you coming out of the Grizzly Peak Grill."

Charles patted his wife's shoulder. "We were surprised at how many people were on Main Street, but we assumed they were all tourists like us."

"I was running some errands for the inn and had lunch at Gran's Café with Becky. Did you enjoy your meal at the Grill?"

Violet's frown disappeared. "It was delicious. We'll go back for supper tomorrow, won't we, Charles?"

"Whatever you wish, dear." He pushed her chair into the dining room.

While I was waiting for our last guests to arrive, I checked the inn's website. We had two new reservations for September. I confirmed the openings, then checked the messages. Rick and Debbie Walker had updated their information, saying they planned to arrive soon after four o'clock.

It was already five minutes to four. I swung through the kitchen to see how Becky was doing.

"Are the scones ready?"

She nodded, busy weighing some flour. "They're on the buffet. I didn't get a chance to finish setting up, though."

"I'll take care of it." I looked out at the dining

room. Charles and Violet were at one of the round tables talking to Rose. "It looks like Rose has everything in control out there, at least until the Brooks sisters return."

"Betty Ann and Sally Marie? They are a hoot, aren't they?"

"I don't think they made a good impression on Violet and Charles this morning. They were pretty overbearing for our shrinking Violet."

"You don't need to worry." Becky closed the flour bin and got out a container of salt. "The guests always end up getting along, don't they?"

I glanced out at the dining room. Violet was facing my way at the table. She leaned forward as she talked with Rose, then her face contorted into a grimace, as if she had taken a bite of a bitter lemon. But her expression struck me. It was as if she was enjoying the lemon.

Giving myself a mental shake, I hurried to set up the buffet for tea.

I was imagining things. Her expression had to be caused by nothing more sinister than a painful twinge. Who knew what kind of misery she had to endure? I glanced in her direction again. She had relaxed in her chair and the grimace was gone.

I had to change my bedtime reading. My diet of murder mysteries was affecting me.

By four-fifteen the inn's trademark afternoon tea was like a scene out of an English novel.

The conversation was lively and interesting, thanks to Rose. The Thomas family had joined us, and the girls were doing their best to act like adults. At least,

Taylor was. Toni was still glued to her tablet, trying to beat the level of her game.

After Taylor had set her drink and scone on the table where her parents were sitting, she came over to me.

"My mom said I can look at your library after I finish my snack. Can you show it to me?"

"Sure. I have a minute right now if it's okay with your parents."

Terri had heard Taylor's question and gave her daughter a nod.

"Yes!" Taylor's smile was contagious.

"I'll give you a quick tour, then you can explore on your own whenever you have time. It's this way."

I led the way to the large alcove behind the piano to my favorite part of the inn. Bookshelves lined two of the walls and in the third wall, French doors led to the library deck. In the center of the room was a display case with several of Rose's collectible books, and a couple comfortable chairs took up the rest of the space.

"Oh!" Taylor said as she followed me. "I feel like Belle in Beauty and the Beast. All these books!"

"Rose has organized it like most libraries. The non-fiction books are on the far wall and the fiction is on the left." I stepped closer to the shelves. "Agatha Christie's books are here, as well as other authors. All favorites of Rose."

"Someday, I'm going to have a library like this." Taylor's expression was thoughtful. "I'll have to get a job to pay for them all, though."

"You must have books at home."

"Sure. Kid books. My mom and dad always give us books for our birthdays and Christmas."

"There's the start of your library." We started back to the dining room. "You'll treasure those books as you get older and add to the collection when you can."

"Thanks." Taylor grinned at me. "I will."

The atmosphere in the dining room was still perfect as I crossed over to the reception desk. The sisters hadn't arrived back from their day of sight-seeing yet, but they had said they might not return until after supper.

I crossed my fingers.

I genuinely liked Betty Ann and Sally Marie, but the peace we were enjoying now would be over the moment they stepped across the threshold. Quiet didn't seem to be part of their makeup.

When the front door opened, I prepared myself for the onslaught, but it was our newest guests instead.

"Good afternoon," I said to the older couple. "You must be Rick and Debbie Walker."

"That's right." Rick smiled at me, his gray beard unable to hide his engaging expression. "We're sorry we're late, but we hadn't expected the Dignity statue in Chamberlain to be so captivating."

"Have you seen it?" Debbie asked. When I shook my head, she went on. "It is beautiful and conveys the spirit of the Native Americans perfectly in the graceful lines of the woman. Like a dancer captured in motion."

Her hands flew as she spoke as if she was trying to express the movement the statue could only represent. Her gently curled silver hair with strands of gold lowlights added to the ethereal quality of her description.

"I'm sorry." She laughed as her hands dropped to her side like birds coming to roost on a branch. "I get carried away sometimes." She shook her head as she laughed again.

Rick signed the guest register. "My wife is an artist herself, and her enthusiasm spills over whenever a sculpture or painting catches her imagination."

"An artist?" I turned toward Debbie. "What is your medium?"

"Watercolor illustrations." She handed me a postcard with a picture I recognized.

"That's Billy Blue Bear!" The little brown bear in the blue shirt was one of my favorite children's book characters. "You're that Debbie Walker?"

Rick gave his wife an adorable look of pride. "Writer and illustrator. That little bear is her life."

I passed my hand over the picture of the happy bear. "Someday, if I ever have children, the Billy Blue Bear books are going to be the first I buy for them."

Debbie's hands fluttered. "Oh, my dear, why wait? I have a copy of the first book in our car. It's a gift from me to you."

"That is very generous of you, but I couldn't accept it. At this point, I'm not sure I'm ever going to get married, let alone have children someday."

"Even dreams that seem hopeless need to be dreamed. The book is for you. If you have a child someday, you can share it with him or her. But until then, it is all yours."

A smile took hold even through the emotions I was trying to control. "Do your children enjoy the stories?"

Her eyes grew moist. "The young readers of the world are the only children I have."

I sighed. "Not all dreams come true."

She shook her head. "But that doesn't stop us from dreaming, does it?"

Rick cleared his throat.

"I'm sorry. I didn't mean to go off on a rabbit trail." I took the credit card Rick handed me and inserted it into the card reader. "We are serving tea in the dining room right now, but there is still time to settle into your room before you join us. It is a great way to meet the other guests."

Debbie turned toward the dining area but stopped as if she had seen a ghost. "I can't believe it." She lifted one hand to her throat. "The woman in the wheelchair looks like someone I used to know." She shook her head. "But no. It can't be. She died years ago."

Rick grasped her elbow. "Are you okay?"

She gave him a shaky smile. "Don't worry about me. It was only a bit of a shock. I hadn't thought about Letty since she died, and seeing this woman brings back memories."

The front door opened, and I looked up to see Dave and Joy Albert. I introduced the two couples and they walked into the dining room, chatting as they got acquainted.

Terri came over to me as her daughters set their dishes on the counter.

"That was a wonderful refreshment. Did I see on the website that you serve tea every afternoon?"

"It's Rose's idea. She says everyone needs a sit-down and a spot of tea at the end of the day."

"It's perfect. The girls are rejuvenated and ready to do something, even after traveling all day. We were thinking of going for a walk. Do you have any suggestions?"

"Graves' Gulch Road is a popular place to hike." I led the way to the inn's front door and opened it. "You can see that the road goes on up into the hills after it passes the inn. About a quarter of a mile up there is a gate across the road, but that is only marking the Forest Service boundary. If you take the trail on the left, it will lead you past Graves' Folly, the old mine, and on up to the overlook. Or you could take the path around the gate and continue up the road as far as you would like to go."

She smiled. "That sound perfect. Do you think we'll see any wildlife?"

"I often see deer this time of the afternoon, and there are wild turkeys. You also might see some chipmunks or squirrels."

"Ted," she called to her husband. "Bring the girls and we'll go for a walk."

Ted had picked up the menu from the Grizzly Peak Grill earlier and he held it up. "Is this place within walking distance? The address is in Paragon."

"Yes, it is. If you follow Graves' Gulch Road down the hill and cross the highway, you'll come to Main Street. Turn left and the Grill is only a few shops down on the left side."

Ted and Terri gathered the girls and set off on their adventure while I wandered back to the dining room. I had just taken the Thomas family's dishes from the buffet to the kitchen sink when my phone rang.

"Hey, Cal."

Becky looked up from the block of butter she was cutting into cubes.

"Hey, yourself. We're still waiting on the final lab

work, but the cause of Caro Lewis' death was pretty obvious once our coroner got her on the table."

"That was quick."

Becky mouthed the word, what? I angled my phone away from my ear so we could both hear what Cal was saying.

"It was quick because it was simple. You were right. She died of a heart attack. We're ruling it an unattended death from natural causes, and the case is closed. The gag order is off since I couldn't find any next of kin to notify."

"So, not murder."

"It doesn't look like it." Cal cleared his throat. "The only thing the coroner questioned was an unusually high level of nicotine in her system."

"Nicotine?"

"Yup. But the cause of death is still clear. You can tell Becky to relax. There won't be any official murder investigation."

"Hmm."

"What?" Cal's voice was impatient.

"You said 'official.' Does that mean you think it's suspicious?"

He sighed. "No. I only meant the department isn't investigating."

"What about you?"

"Like I said, the department isn't investigating. Goodbye, Emma."

I hung up the phone and turned back to Becky. "You heard what he said?"

"I heard everything." She dumped the butter cubes into a mixing bowl. "No murder and no case. Cal must be bummed."

I leaned against the prep counter and stuck my

phone in my back pocket. "Something doesn't seem right, though."

"Why?"

"Cal said there was nicotine in Caro's system. How did it get there? Caro was a health nut. I can't imagine her being a smoker."

"Maybe she vaped or used those e-cigarettes."

"I think we would have seen the equipment for either one of those in her gallery or in the back room. I only found healthy snacks and bottled water."

Becky put her elbows on the counter across from me and leaned her chin in her hand. "Then where did the nicotine come from?"

That was a good question.

Four

On Saturday morning, Becky fixed a bread pudding with caramel syrup for breakfast. I had been anticipating it ever since she said it was going to be the Saturday morning staple.

I started the coffee urn on my way through the dining room, then popped into the kitchen to grab a cup of Dark Canyon's Rattlesnake Roast. It was a good thing Becky and I shared a taste for the strong coffee, even if she did dress hers up with a ton of sugar and cream.

"I'm glad you're here," Becky said. "Gran called and she needs my help."

"In the café?"

"No, with the parade float." She slid a baking dish into the oven and set the timer. "Jeremy broke his collarbone this morning."

"Poor guy." Nine-year-old Jeremy was my favorite of Becky's cousin's boys.

"He's going to be okay, but my cousin had to take him to the hospital to get it x-rayed." She turned to me as she set her hot mitts on the prep counter. "The problem is that it leaves the parade float without a foreman, and I'm next up."

"I almost forgot the parade is this morning." I took a sip of my coffee. The aroma of cinnamon from the bread pudding mingled with the fragrance of the coffee. Even before the caffeine hit, I felt like I could take on anything. "What do you need me to do?"

Becky grinned. "I knew I could count on you." She started untying her apron. "The bread pudding comes out of the oven at six-forty-five. You let it rest for fifteen minutes before you cut it into serving pieces. Got it?"

"Fifteen minutes."

"There is caramel sauce on the stove. You'll need to stir it once in a while. Put the servings of the bread pudding on plates, then drizzle the warm caramel on just before you serve it. There's a fruit salad in the fridge and muffins in the warmer. The muffins need to go in a basket on the buffet." She took off her hair net and put it in the pocket of her apron. "But the most important thing is the cookies."

"Cookies? For breakfast?"

She showed me a pastry box on the back counter. "Anna Grace over at Living Wild ordered these for her grand opening today. They need to be delivered at nine-thirty."

"Nine-thirty. Got it."

"And then you'll be right there to watch the parade go by." Becky waved, partway out the door already. "Thanks, Emma. You're a lifesaver."

Breakfast went smoothly. The Brooks sisters entertained Taylor and Toni with stories from when they were girls, and the other guests compared notes on which tourist spots they were planning to see. By eight-thirty they had all gone to Paragon to get a good spot to watch the parade.

Rose helped me load the dishwasher and clean the kitchen before I left to deliver the cookies.

"Have you heard any more about Caro Lewis' death?" she asked as she ran water into the three-compartment sink.

"Cal called last night and said she died of a heart attack." I loaded the plates into the dishwasher.

"Not a murder?"

"He doesn't think so."

Rose set the baking pan in the soapy water and turned toward me. "But you have your doubts."

It wasn't a question. Yes, I had doubts about Cal's opinion and Rose could tell.

"He said the coroner found high levels of nicotine in her blood, but she didn't use tobacco."

"Nicotine."

Again, it wasn't a question. Rose's expression was thoughtful.

"What do you know about nicotine?" I asked.

"I've known it to be used as a poison, but it isn't common." She thrust her hands into the dishwater and started scrubbing the pan. "The delivery method isn't certain, and the fatal amount varies depending on the victim. Unless the murderer used enough of it to ensure death..." Her voice trailed off.

Sometimes Rose's experience as an international spy gave me more information than I needed.

"Do you really think someone could have poisoned Caro with nicotine?" I closed the dishwasher and started it. "And wouldn't the coroner have brought that possibility up if there was enough nicotine in her system to kill her?"

Rose rinsed the baking pan. "You're right of

course. He would have told Cal if he thought her death was suspicious. But I have to wonder."

I checked the time. It was nine-fifteen and time for me to take the cookies to Living Wild. I hung up my apron and grabbed the box of cookies.

"Are you going to the parade?" I asked.

"I wouldn't miss it."

"I'll see you there."

As I headed out the door and down the hill toward town, I could see the parade entries lining up along Church Street near the school and park. I hurried to get to Living Wild on time.

A bell above the door tinkled as I went in. Anna Grace was arranging figurines on a shelf. The little birds were made to look like they had been carved out of stone, and she was placing them among ivy leaves. I stopped to admire one that looked like a wren.

"They look like pieces from a Victorian English country house," I said. My minimalist lifestyle didn't leave much room for decorations, but I wondered how one would look in my suite now that I didn't expect to move to a new location every few years.

"That's the idea," the store owner said with a smile. "I try to choose decorations that bring nature into our homes."

"That's where you got the name of your store. It's perfect. I brought the cookies you ordered."

I set the box on the cashier stand and looked around. The walls were papered to look like a grove of aspen trees and gave the impression that I was walking through a forest. Along with the birds, Anna Grace had displays of other woodland creatures, greenery, some intriguing prints of leaves and ferns, beautiful napkins and kitchen linens, and signs that said things like, "Life is better at the cabin."

"Thanks," she said. "I hope others feel the same way you do."

The petite store owner was about my age, perhaps a few years older, with light brown hair in a messy bun, and dark eyes. I hadn't had a chance to chat with her when I had stopped by to drop off the brochures the previous afternoon, so I welcomed these few minutes to get to know her better.

"This weekend is your grand opening?"

Anna Grace's brow dipped in a worried V. "I opened a couple weeks ago, and business has been trickling in. I'm hoping the crowds here for Paragon Days will help make a big splash."

"Don't worry. Between your great displays and Becky's cookies, they'll be here."

She looked relieved. "Do you think so?"

"Prop the front door open after the parade and the customers will stream in."

"I hope you're right." She hesitated. "I don't know if you've heard, but we've had a death in town."

"Yes. Caro Lewis." I noticed her eyes were moist. "Did you know her well?"

"No. It's only that every sudden death brings back memories of the day I lost my husband." She blew her nose and laughed a little. "You know, I didn't even like Caro. She was very condescending when she visited my store."

"Did she ask you about her art colony idea?"

"She walked in here, said something about plebeian ideas of decor, then asked me to donate my space for a studio so she could expand her art gallery." She dabbed at her eyes, but the emotional reaction was over. "As if I thought her art colony scheme was worth giving up Living Wild." She cast a loving glance around the store. "I invested Dan's life insurance money and a big chunk of our savings in this place, and she thought I would just hand it over to her."

"That was pretty bold of her."

Anna Grace nodded. "I thought so, too. She said since my business was new, I could start again in another town. But that isn't possible, even if I wanted to. I'd lose all my equity and miss most of the season's business."

I considered what Caro had asked. Only an extremely thoughtless and selfish person would think Anna Grace would accept the idea.

A rattle of drums sounded from outside.

"It sounds like the parade is starting," I said. "Are you planning to watch it?"

"I love parades." She stowed an empty box behind the cashier stand. "We can watch from the sidewalk in front of the store."

A row of Gran's great-grandchildren was lined up on the curb in front of Living Wild, but we found a place to stand behind them. Down the block, Cal's Deputy SUV led the parade. He drove slowly, waving at the crowd. When he reached us, he sounded his siren and the kids cheered. He gave me a wave as he drove by.

Next came the drummers I had heard, followed by the color guard carrying the flags. Then the floats started. Gran's Café was first. It featured an ancient wood stove with Gran standing at it, flipping pancakes. All the family who wasn't watching the parade stood or sat on the float. I waved at Becky, and she threw a piece of candy my way.

Then they had moved on and the next float was coming. This one was from a business outside of town offering helicopter rides. The next one was advertising Hogs and Suds. I waved to Billy and Barb as they rode their motorcycles behind the float.

I looked down the street and counted at least ten more floats, plus groups walking along. It seemed like every resident of the town was in the parade, and the sidewalks were still filled with spectators.

By ten-thirty the last of the parade went by, with Cal's SUV following the final float. He must have circled around to close the parade the same way he had opened it.

"That was fun," Anna Grace said, "but I had better get back inside."

There was already a crowd of tourists looking in her store window.

"Have a great day," I said, and started walking back to the inn past Come on Up.

"Hi there," a young woman said as she propped the front door open. "You stopped by yesterday afternoon and talked with Jack, my husband. I'm Shasta."

"I'm Emma." I stepped out of the line of sidewalk traffic. "You were busy with customers yesterday. It looks like an exciting start to the season."

"It sure is." Shasta smiled. She wore hiking clothes and looked like a living advertisement for their store. "I love all the excitement of the parade, and folks flock to town to see it."

"And stick around to shop?"

She grinned. "That's the idea. By the way, a few of the guests from the inn stopped by already this morning looking for maps and trail guides. Thanks for sending them our way."

"I'm glad they found you. I don't know much about the trails in the area, but I knew you would have the information they needed."

Down the street, a group of people were gathered outside the art gallery.

Shasta frowned. "It looks like they're getting upset."

"The gallery is closed, isn't it?"

"That's what the sign says."

I walked over to see what was going on. There was a half-dozen people in the group, and none of them were happy.

"I agree," a young woman was saying. "If the art show is canceled, where are the pieces that were going to be displayed?"

"And what about our entry fees?" This was from a big man with a leather vest and a ponytail. "How are we going to get our money back?"

"The lawyers will probably take it all," said a thin blond woman with a shrill voice. "Caro Lewis cheated us."

"That's right," someone else said. "She ran out on us with our money."

I stepped into the crowd.

"I think you have the wrong idea. It isn't Caro Lewis' fault she isn't here to open the gallery. She passed away yesterday."

I had expected the news would calm the situation, but they only became more agitated.

"Who is in charge?"

"Where are our entries for the show?"

"What's going to happen?"

An older woman dressed in a bright green

muumuu raised an imperious hand. "I'm sure the authorities will get to the bottom of this fiasco. Meanwhile, perhaps someone will be able to open the gallery. I will oversee the viewing and sales of any items that are purchased."

This was getting out of hand.

"You'll need to speak to the police before you do anything," I said.

The woman turned her gaze to me. "Why? These talented artists are the ones who own the property inside the gallery, so they should have access to it. I say the show and sale should go on as Ms. Lewis planned." She turned to the crowd. "Does anyone have a key to the door?"

Pony-tail guy stepped forward, a set of lock-picking tools in his hand. "We don't need a key."

I stepped away from the group and called Cal.

Cal showed up at the art gallery in his SUV, lights flashing.

"Hey, folks," he said as he walked over to the group on the sidewalk. "What's going on?"

Pony-tail guy hid his lock-picking tools in his hand as he straightened up and turned to face the deputy.

"We were waiting for Caro to open the gallery, then this lady showed up and told us she was dead." He thrust a thumb in my direction. "We only wanted to go on with the art show."

The lady in the green muumuu gave Cal a smile and put a purr in her voice. "It's what Caro would have wanted, don't you think?"

The rest of the group agreed with her as Cal made his way to the door and planted himself between it and the artists.

"I understand your frustration, but we can't open the gallery at this time. It is the scene of an unattended death and hasn't been cleared yet."

The blond lady pushed herself forward. "What about my art? It's languishing in the negative energy flow from Caro's transition to the other side. Who knows what vibes my babies will pick up?"

Cal exchanged glances with me.

"We'll try to settle this as soon as possible, but for now-"

"Is it going to be today?" That was from a young man in a black t-shirt. "If not, we'll take care of it ourselves. It's our property, not yours."

Cal's expression didn't change. "We need to do things legally. I'll try to get this investigation wrapped up today, but I can't promise anything." He took a step forward. "Now, if you folks would please move along. There is plenty to do in town. Enjoy yourselves while you let me do my work."

No one moved.

"All right. Stay here. But if the gallery is disturbed, I will bring all of you up on charges of trespassing."

At that, most of the group moved along toward the park at the edge of town, but pony-tail guy stayed where he was.

"How can it be trespassing when the items in the gallery are our property?" he asked.

"Because the gallery isn't your property," Cal said. "Please be patient with the authorities. I'll let you know when you can retrieve your belongings from the building."

Pony-tail guy crossed his arms and took Cal's place in front of the door.

Cal sighed. "By the way, your lock picks are legal unless or until you use them to commit a crime."

"What lock picks?"

"Just FYI."

Cal motioned for me to climb in his SUV.

"Do you think he's going to try to break in?" I asked as I fastened my seat belt.

Putting the SUV in gear, Cal eased into the traffic lane. "I wouldn't doubt it. I had a run-in with Moose earlier in the week, and he isn't the type to let a little thing like trespassing laws stop him."

"Moose?"

"Yup. Moose Morehead."

"That's his real name?"

"It's what Mom and Dad Morehead named their little boy. I ran a full background check on him." He cut a sideways glance at me as he turned the corner at the convenience store. "And before you ask, no, I can't share the details with you."

"What happened last week?"

Cal turned onto Church Street and drove slowly back toward the other end of town past the residential houses.

"He was disturbing the peace. Arguing with one of the other customers at Hogs and Suds."

"I wouldn't peg him as one of Caro's artists."

"He does those nuts-and-bolts sculptures. Mostly motorcycles."

I remembered seeing them in the gallery.

Cal turned the corner on Maggie Street, then into the alley behind the art gallery. He put the car in park and unfastened his seatbelt.

"Now we wait," he said.

"For what?"

He stared at the back door of the gallery. "Just wait." He tapped the steering wheel with one finger. "Whatever happens, you stay in the vehicle. Got it?"

I nodded and rolled the window down. I'd stay in the SUV, but I didn't want to miss out on the action.

After about ten minutes, someone pushed the gallery door open with a black-booted foot. Cal hit the button to sound the siren once, then jumped out and yanked the gallery door all the way open.

Moose Morehead stumbled out of the doorway, a box piled with his sculptures in his arms. He tried to run, but the bulky box got in his way. Cal grabbed one elbow and led him over to the SUV.

"Well, Moose. I guess you didn't take my advice."

He set the box on the ground and turned the big man so he was facing the hood of the vehicle.

"I was only recovering my property," Moose said, trying to turn toward Cal.

"Come on. You know the drill. Hands on the hood, feet spread."

Cal patted him down and removed a knife from a holder tucked in his belt. He also took the lock picks. Then he handcuffed Moose and put him in the back of the SUV. That's when I got out. Cal handed me a pair of gloves and pulled on his own pair.

"What did he take from the store?" I pulled one of the sculptures out of the box.

Cal picked up another one. "It looks like he took his own artwork like he said."

Underneath the metal conglomerations, there was a solid piece of cardboard at the bottom of the box.

"Does the bottom look a little hinky to you?" I asked.

"Yup. The depth of the inside of the box doesn't

match the outside." Cal reached in to remove the cardboard. Underneath there was a layer of plastic.

Moose started kicking the inside of the SUV. "Leave my stuff alone!"

Neither of us paid attention to him as Cal reached in and pulled out the plastic bundle. Inside the layers of clear wrapping were smaller packages of beige powder.

Moose yelled again. "Hey, that's not mine! I've never seen that before!"

"Is that what I think it is?" I had never seen a package of drugs in person, but I had watched plenty of mystery and crime shows on television.

Cal hefted the package in his hand. "With that color, I'm guessing fentanyl. I'll need to have the lab tell me for sure, but I have enough evidence to arrest him for trespassing and hold him while we see if there are other charges."

"Where did he get it? He didn't have anything like this when we were all in front of the gallery."

"He had to have taken it from inside. Maybe Caro had hidden it somewhere that he knew about."

"But where did Caro get it?"

Cal got his duffel from the SUV and took out his camera. "That's where my investigation comes in." He snapped pictures of the box, the package, and the sculptures before he put everything back.

"Could Moose and Caro have been in on the drugs together?"

I stripped off my gloves and followed as he carried the box to the back of the SUV and opened the rear hatch.

"That's a possibility." His tone was noncommittal.

I waited until he shut Moose's yelling protests

inside the SUV again while the scenario raced through my mind.

"That could be why Caro was buying artwork from China." I followed him to the driver's side door. "Somewhere along the route, the drug smugglers put the packages of drugs in the cartons, and then they would be delivered here where Caro would pass them on to Moose. He'd sell them and they'd split the profits."

Cal leaned on the door without opening it. We both ignored Moose's muffled raging.

"You've been watching detective shows on television again, haven't you?"

I could blame him for my television habit, but this wasn't the time or place to ask him why he hadn't called me.

"Those detective shows are based on facts."

His eyes narrowed.

"Well," I said, backing down a bit. "Loosely based on facts."

"Look." Cal took a toothpick out of his pocket and stuck it in the corner of his mouth. "The scenario you described is plausible. I'll look into it."

He reached for the door handle.

"Wait," I said, grabbing his arm. "Maybe that's why Caro was murdered. Something went wrong with the drug deal and Moose killed her."

He let go of the door handle and gave me his "deputy look."

"Caro's death was from natural causes. She wasn't murdered."

"What about the high level of nicotine in her blood?"

"Somehow, she was exposed to a high

concentration of nicotine." He leaned against the SUV. "Between you and me, I think the nicotine is suspicious, too. But I think suicide is more likely than homicide."

"Suicide by nicotine?"

"That's the angle I'm looking at. In my investigation, I found out she had a heart condition. One that had been with her since a childhood bout of rheumatic fever, but it was getting worse as she got older. I figure she couldn't face not knowing when her heart would fail, so she decided to hurry things along."

"With nicotine?"

"The high dose could cause a heart attack, which is what killed her."

I considered Cal's idea. "But why now? Right before the opening of the art show she had worked so hard to organize?"

"I can't see into her state of mind at the time of her death."

"How would you prove she committed suicide?"

"That's the problem. I can't. It's going to take some digging to find out more about her." He gave me another piercing look. "But I'm going to be doing the digging, not you. This is still an ongoing investigation."

"With the complication of the drugs."

Cal opened the door and sat in the driver's seat. The plastic partition between the front and the back didn't mute Moose's rant as well as the closed vehicle had.

"I'll be sending a team in to search for more evidence. But remember, Emma," Cal said through the open door. "It's my investigation. You take care of the guests at the inn."

He closed the door and drove to the other end of the alley. The tires spun in the gravel as he turned toward the highway.

I kicked at the ground, sending a shower of loose stones after him. He wanted me to mind my own business? After the help I had given him in the last murder investigation? And after he hadn't called for the past month?

The sounds from the after-parade crowds on Main Street drifted into the alley, along with the fragrance of frying dough. I took a deep breath, tempted by the funnel cakes, but put them out of my mind.

Caro Lewis was dead. And there were drugs involved, which made it a crime whether Cal's suicide theory was correct or not.

I followed the alley to the end of the block. I had work to do at the inn. My mind worked better when my hands were busy, and there was a lot of thinking to do. Cal's theory didn't make sense. Caro had worked too hard to create the art gallery, plus the art colony idea wasn't even off the ground yet. She was creating a future, not regretting a past.

I stopped at the corner by Gran's Café and looked back at the gallery. Next to it was the old-time photo shop. The two storefronts looked identical except for the colorful paint job on Caro's place.

What made her choose Paragon for her art colony? I continued toward the inn. We would probably never know.

Five

Possible murder or not, we still had a bed and breakfast to run.

Making my way from room to room, I made beds, changed towels, and vacuumed. I mused about how much I learned about a person from how they left their rooms in the morning, knowing a maid would be in later. As I was finishing up in the Thomas family's suite, I heard the Brooks sisters talking in the second-floor lounge.

"I'm going to take my knitting to the porch." That was Sally Marie's voice. "Do you want to bring your new word search puzzle book?"

"That's a good idea," Betty Ann said, "but it's almost time for supper, isn't it? Look at my watch."

"We just had lunch. It's only a little after noon."

"No, it isn't. Look at my watch. It's nearly five o'clock."

"Let me see." A pause. "Betty Ann, you goofball, you set your watch two hours ahead instead of two hours back. It isn't even one o'clock yet. Let me fix it for you."

"It isn't supper time yet?"

"No, dear. We have all afternoon to relax."

"Can we go see Mount Rushmore tomorrow?"

"Do you remember how Daddy always wanted to visit it? He would be tickled pink to know we're actually going to see it."

I heard them next as they started down the stairs.

"Do you think the little doggie will visit us on the porch again?"

"He might. Did you remember your tissues?"

"I have them in my pocket."

I finished up the Snow Goose and locked the door behind me. The conversation I had overheard sounded normal for the sisters, but it seemed odd to me that at their ages Sally Marie treated Betty Ann like a child. A life-time habit? Or did Betty Ann need the constant supervision?

I gather up the load of soiled towels and went downstairs to the laundry. The Summerwine suite, where Violet and Charles were staying, had a "do not disturb" sign hanging from the door lever, so I went ahead and started the washer. I heard Becky in the kitchen.

"Hi, Becks," I said, pushing the swinging door open. "How did the parade go?"

"Tons of fun and then some." She grinned. "Did you enjoy it?"

"I was surprised at how many floats there were. I didn't realize there were that many people in town."

"That's the summer season for you." Becky slipped her apron over her head and tied it in back. "Once the tourists arrive, the town starts rockin'. And Paragon Days is only the beginning."

"Are these crowds normal?"

"Until the middle of August. When schools start up again, the families stop coming. We have some shoulder-season tourists until the end of October, but the official end of the season is Labor Day."

"What are shoulder-season tourists?"

Becky reached into the cooler and brought out butter and milk and set them on the prep counter. "That's what they call late spring and early fall visitors. Retirees and other folks who don't have kids in school are free to travel when they want, so a lot of them choose to visit when it isn't as crowded."

"It must be a northern thing. At the hotels where I've worked the busy months were on the corporations' schedules, not families."

"I can't imagine many families vacationed in St. Kitts." Becky went back to the cooler for a carton of eggs and an orange.

"You'd be surprised how many do, but you're right. Not as many as here in the Black Hills."

Becky measured flour into a bowl, then added baking soda. "Now what? You're just hanging around the inn this afternoon? I thought you had a murder to investigate."

"Cal is investigating, but he hasn't committed to the idea of a murder. We did find a drug connection this morning, though."

"And he still doesn't think her death is a murder?"

"Not yet. He's going to look into her background and see if anything comes to the surface."

I heard a noise from the dining room. The overhead shutters on the buffet counter were closed, but I peeked through the door to see if anyone needed me. It was Charles and Violet. Her wheelchair was by the tea and coffee station while Charles set two cups of tea on a tray in her lap. Violet saw me and nodded, but her expression was dour.

"Can I help you with anything?" I asked.

"No, thank you," Charles said. He turned his wife's wheelchair toward their suite. "We're going to spend some time relaxing after our busy morning."

I let the door close and went back to my conversation with Becky.

"Why aren't you looking into her background?" she asked.

"Cal said he would do it. He really doesn't want me messing with his investigation."

"He didn't want you messing with the last one, but without you-"

"And you," I put in.

"Yup, that's right. Without us, he never would have solved that case."

"Well, I guess I could do a search for her name on the internet and see what pops up."

Becky's eyes glowed. "I think that's a great idea. We'll do it this evening. I'll bring a pizza."

The rest of the afternoon went quickly as I finished up my work, and soon the guests were arriving for tea. Rose came out of her suite with Thatcher.

"Did you get a lot of work done?" I asked her.

Rose spent her days writing her memoirs. I had hoped her book would be published soon, but Rose had made it clear the story of her career with the World Intelligence Organization would remain private until after her death.

She tucked a stray strand of hair under her sun hat. "It has proven to be a more difficult task than I had anticipated. Remembering details from the past can be comforting at times, but other memories are quite unsettling." She smiled. "But yes, I made good progress today."

Thatcher jumped up on my knee and I stooped to pet him. Rose leaned closer.

"Did you make any progress on the death?"

"I think it's murder, but Cal doesn't think so."

"He won't commit until he finds evidence."

"Or a motive." I held Thatcher's face between my hands and rubbed his ears as his eyes closed in ecstasy. "Becky and I are going to see what we can learn about Caro through an internet search tonight."

"Let me know if you need any help." Rose started toward the door and Thatcher abandoned me to run ahead of her.

After Rose left, Betty Ann and Sally Marie came in from the porch. They helped themselves to the iced tea I had set on the buffet, and each took an orange scone.

"I must have the recipe for these," Sally Marie said after her first bite.

"I'll have to ask Becky if she's willing to share it," I said.

"The icing is delicious. They are more like cakes than biscuits, aren't they, Betty Ann?"

"Like Mama used to make." Sally Marie's words were muffled as she took another bite.

"Mama never made anything like these." Betty Ann frowned as she examined the scone in her hand. "But the flavor is familiar. I can't tell why."

"Remember Mama's hummingbird cake?" Sally Marie sipped her tea. "She put orange zest in the frosting, just like these have."

"That's right!" Betty Ann beamed. "Mama's hummingbird cake." She sighed. "I've never been able to make it as well as she could."

The rest of the guests dribbled in and joined the group in the dining room. From the conversations I overheard, they had spent the day in Paragon shopping after watching the parade.

After they had all left to enjoy their evening plans, Becky and I met in my suite. She had picked up a pizza from the convenience store in town and Thatcher had followed her up the stairs.

I broke off a piece of crust and gave it to him. "Come on in, pup. Tim will enjoy the furry company."

The corgi jumped onto the sectional and touched noses with Tim in a greeting, then flopped over, tongue lolling in a smile.

"It's like he understands what we're doing and doesn't want to miss any of it," I said as I set my laptop on the big ottoman next to the pizza.

"Of course," Becky said. She joined me on the couch after picking up a couple napkins from the kitchen. "He knows we're working on a case and wants to be in on it."

I smiled at her comment but didn't say anything. If Becky wanted to give Thatcher credit for more intelligence than a normal dog would possess, I wouldn't get in the way. After all, he had saved my life as well as Rose's in our last case.

I brought up the search engine and typed in Caro's name. Several hits came up. I took a bite of pizza as I scrolled through them.

"What's that?" Becky said. She pointed to one headline. "It's from the Forestgreen Art Academy. Isn't that a famous school in Chicago?"

I clicked on it. "It looks like a publicity blurb from when Caro retired." I put my slice of pizza down.

"She had been a student there in the 1970s, and won a prize for her painting, *Almost Spring*, which hung in the Chicago Art Museum until a couple of years ago. After she graduated, she was hired as a teacher in the Modern Art department, and several of her students went on to have successful careers as artists."

"Hmm. It doesn't say anything about the rest of her career as an artist. Did she stop painting?"

"Artists and writers often have a website to show the portfolio of their work." I went back to the results of my search. "Here's her website."

I clicked on the link. The site featured the prize-winning painting, but the other paintings she listed were similar to the ones I had seen on display in her art gallery. It seemed the website's main purpose was to advertise her availability for artist in residence programs and interim teaching positions. I clicked on the link to the page labeled Paragon.

"This page has been added recently." I scrolled through the photos. "See? These are photos from this weekend's art show at the gallery. She must have taken them earlier this week, after she set up the displays."

"What about that page?" Becky pointed to the website menu. "The one labeled 'About Caro.' That should tell us more."

The page had a publicity shot of Caro, looking much younger than the woman we had met, and a short biography. When she had been born, her schooling, and highlights of her career as a teacher.

"Nothing about her other paintings."

"She was a one hit wonder." Becky opened a can of flavored carbonated water. "It doesn't look like we're going to learn much more from her website."

"Let's do a search for her name." I went back to the search results and scrolled through the rest of the hits. "Nothing new here."

"Try her full name. Probably Caroline?"

I typed it in and started scrolling. Again, nothing new. I went on to the second page, and then the third.

"There!" Becky pointed to one of the listings. "Try that one. It's from the early 70s, but her age would be right."

The link was to a newspaper archive. I clicked on it and read the first line aloud. "Caroline Lewis, twenty-three, was arrested Thursday for cultivating marijuana plants with the intent to distribute."

Becky looked at me. "She was a drug dealer."

"Maybe, but these are misdemeanor charges. She didn't even do jail time." I pointed to the line about her receiving a suspended sentence.

"Still, if she was involved in drugs back then, doesn't it make sense she might have continued?"

"And gotten into the hard stuff? She didn't look like a drug user."

"Maybe she didn't take the drugs." Becky shrugged. "Just because you sell the stuff doesn't mean you're addicted to it."

I closed the laptop. "We can mention it to Cal. If there's anything there, he'll find it."

"I could smell the fragrance of that bacon cooking from upstairs," I said as I walked into the kitchen on Sunday morning. "What are you making?"

"I'm trying a recipe I found on the internet," Becky said. She was rolling out dough on the island.

"It's bacon and cheese wrapped in pastry. Kind of like a savory apple turnover."

"Without the apples?" I poured myself a cup of coffee.

Becky's rolling pin stopped, suspended over the sheet of dough on the counter. "You gave me a fabulous idea. Bacon, cheddar cheese, and apples." She grinned. "What do you think?"

"Apples with bacon and cheese?" I inhaled the steam from the coffee as I considered it. "Why not? Sounds interesting."

"I have some Granny Smiths in the fridge. I'll slice them and cook them up like an apple pie filling." She went back to her rolling. "I can make half of the turnovers with apples and half without. We'll see what the guests think."

"Are you using pie crust? It looks like puff pastry."

"Puff pastry is my go-to for most dishes like this."

"You know most people buy it in a box at the grocery store."

"Most people aren't professional bakers."

I laughed. "Now you're beginning to sound like Wil."

She shuddered. "Sorry. It won't happen again."

"What are we having with the turnovers?"

"Berry fruit cups and scrambled eggs." She gave the pastry a last flourish with her rolling pin, then picked up a pizza wheel. "I'll cook the eggs in small batches, so they don't have to sit in the chafing rack for long. There's nothing worse than rubbery eggs."

I could think of a lot of things that were worse, but she was right about the eggs.

Becky cut the pastry into squares with the pizza wheel. "We never got around to making our crime board last night. If we have a murder on our hands, we'll need one."

"You think it's a murder, too? I'm not the only one?"

"From what you've told me, something suspicious is going on in this town." She started arranging bacon slices diagonally on the squares but pointed one at me as she continued. "Paragon may be a small town, but it's my town. I don't want drugs or murder or any kind of crime to happen here."

I thought for a minute as she went back to building the turnovers.

"We already have that kind of crime here, Becky. There isn't much we can do to keep it out."

"But we can make sure the bad guys don't get away with it." Her voice was a growl. "Look at what we did last month. Without our clue-hunting and crime-solving work, Wil might have gotten away with making this area into a uranium mine."

"That wasn't a crime, you know."

"It should be. And the murders he committed were. But we stopped him."

I grinned. "We did, didn't we?"

"So, it's a deal? I'll find a piece of poster board, you bring the markers, and we'll set up the crime lab in your suite this afternoon." She finished laying out the bacon slices and picked up a bowl of shredded cheddar cheese. "Make sure Thatcher joins us, and Tim. I'm not entirely convinced Thatcher didn't understand everything we were talking about last night. And I'm sure Tim can read."

"They are a dog and a cat."

Becky shrugged. "They are still part of the team."

I left Becky to her breakfast prep and went into

the dining room to start the coffee for the guests then stepped outside to get the newspaper. The sun was beginning to come over the top of Grizzly Peak and its rays lit the front of the inn with brilliant light. The climbing roses on either side of the inn's entrance were beginning to leaf out, promising a gorgeous display in the coming months. It looked like summer at the Sweetbrier was going to be amazing.

Cal's SUV turned off the highway below and started climbing up Graves' Gulch Road toward the inn. I waited until he parked on the concrete apron in front of the garage door, then walked over to meet my favorite deputy.

He rolled his window down.

"Hey," I said. "This is an early stop for you."

"I'm on my way to the office before church, but I have some news for you. After further tests, the coroner decided the nicotine in Caro's system was the cause of her heart attack."

"I was right. It was murder."

"Not necessarily. Only if the nicotine overdose was administered with the intent of killing her."

"What else could it be?"

"Accidental."

"Accidental? When we know drugs were involved?"

"It could be. Remember, I'm the one who keeps the facts in mind." He grinned at me. Actually grinned.

"While I don't?"

"You tend to make the facts fit into some mystery story scenario."

I frowned at him. "What's wrong with that?"

"Sometimes you go down the wrong path. I can't

afford to go chasing down rabbit trails every time you and my cousin start spinning your theories." He drummed on the steering wheel with his thumbs.

"Have you found out anything about Caro's background?"

He shook his head. "Nothing more than what we already knew. How about you?"

I took a step back. "You made it very clear I was - how did you put it? - supposed to take care of the guests at the inn and leave the investigating to you."

"I know you, Emma. If there was a way to find out anything, you would dig it up no matter what I said."

I studied the toes of my shoes.

"I'm right, aren't I?"

I gave in. "We found an article on-line from fifty years ago. Caro had been arrested for growing marijuana with intent to distribute."

"Fifty years ago?"

"That doesn't mean she isn't still involved in the drug trade." I shifted my gaze toward the garage to avoid looking straight into the blinding early morning sun. "She was probably an aging hippie that never got over her flower child days."

"But we have no evidence the drugs we found were hers. My money is on Moose." Cal stuck the toothpick in the corner of his mouth. "I need to get to the office, but you've given me some things to consider."

"You're going to look further into Caro's background, aren't you?"

"I'm still not convinced her death is murder."

"But something is hinky around here." I put my hand on the door frame as he started the engine. "Wait. Do you know how the nicotine got into Caro's system?"

"There was nicotine residue on the picture that was on the floor next to her. The nicotine was absorbed through her skin."

I shuddered. "It was that easy to do?"

"The coroner's theory was that Caro's heart condition played a big part in her death, since the amount of nicotine CSU found wouldn't be lethal to most people." He pointed his toothpick at me. "This is all confidential, understand?"

I crossed my heart with my finger. "I won't spread it around." I wouldn't tell anyone except Becky and Rose.

"See you at church."

Rose and Thatcher were coming out of the front door as I started back into the inn.

"Good morning," Rose said as she watched Thatcher head toward his corner of the garden. "Was that Cal?"

"He had news about the case. He said the nicotine was definitely the cause of Caro's death."

"Does he think it was intentional?"

I gazed at the dust cloud from Cal's SUV still hanging in the air over the road. "He isn't convinced Caro's death was a murder, but he is looking into her background as much as he can."

"I hope he finds something useful." Rose watched Thatcher sniff the edge of the flower bed. "He has access to more sources than we do. The strong arm of the law and all that."

Later, after church, Becky grabbed me. "We need to ask Cal if we can see the photos he took the other day when you found Caro's body."

"Do you think he'll let us have copies?" We

walked toward the corner of the yard where Cal was talking to some of the young cousins. Jeremy was there with his left arm in a sling.

"If he doesn't think it's murder, then they aren't crime scene photos, right?"

I grinned at her. "That's right. If there's no crime, there's no harm in letting us see the pictures."

"What pictures?" The kids had abandoned Cal for the park playground across the road and he had heard my last comment.

Becky glanced at me. "Emma said you had taken photos at the art gallery the other day. We were wondering if you could send us some copies of them."

He crossed his arms, suddenly looking very official, even out of uniform. "So you can make a crime scene out of the incident?"

I crossed my arms and faced him. "If there wasn't a crime, we can't make one up, can we?"

He raised his eyebrows.

"Okay, we could. But we won't." I abandoned my official police business stance. "But wouldn't it be helpful to have a couple extra pairs of eyes to look through those photos?"

He looked from me to Becky. "You'll need to keep them confidential-"

Becky squealed and gave him a hug. "Thanks Cal, you won't regret it."

"I think I already do." Cal pulled himself out of his cousin's arms. "I'll download them onto a thumb drive and drop it off at the inn."

"Wouldn't email be faster?" I asked.

"Faster, but not as secure."

"Hey, Cal!" One of the kids at the playground

called to him, waving one arm in the air. "Come see this cool bug Jeremy found."

"I'll bring the thumb drive over after lunch," he said as he waved back at the boys. "But first, there are bugs to identify."

"A deputy's job is never done?"

He grinned. "I hope not." He jogged across the road toward the playground.

"Great!" Becky did a fist-pump. "Now we can really get started investigating this murder."

Six

I was beginning to get immersed in Agatha Christie's *Death on the Nile* when a knock sounded on the door of my suite. Becky pushed through the door as soon as I opened it.

"Cal dropped off the thumb drive," she said. "And I got the poster board." Tim bristled at the intrusion and went to hide under my bed as Becky slid the cardboard onto my ottoman. "You have your markers, right? And where's Thatcher?"

"Thatcher is with Rose, in the middle of his afternoon nap." I moved my book out of her way and popped into my bedroom to grab my bag of Bullet Journal supplies and my laptop. "I think we can handle this without our resident corgi." I settled on the couch next to her. "Did Cal say anything about Caro's murder when you saw him?"

She shook her head and started digging through my markers for her favorite purple. "Clammed up like always. Sometimes I can't believe we're related."

I turned on my laptop and inserted the thumb drive. When I opened the file, Becky leaned against me to watch the screen as I scrolled through the photos. The scenes were familiar. When I got to the series Cal had taken of Caro, I slowed down.

"This is the way she was when I found her."

"She looks like she just collapsed." Becky leaned closer and pointed to the screen. "Is that the picture you told me about?"

"Yeah. Cal said there was a nicotine residue on the frame."

"And that's what killed her?"

"I did some research on nicotine. The chemical raises your heart rate and blood pressure, so for someone who has a heart problem, it wouldn't take much of a dose to send her into cardiac arrest."

"She looks like she was pretty fit. Are you sure she had a heart problem?"

"That's what Cal said." I kept scrolling through the photos and stopped on the picture that had been next to Caro's body. "This is weird."

"What?"

"Here." I pointed to the picture. Cal had turned the frame over and had snapped a shot of the front. "This is different from the rest of the stuff in Caro's gallery. It's a picture of leaves." I enlarged the photo.

"It looks like a print that one of our chemistry teachers taught us to do in high school."

"Chemistry?"

"Yeah. You use photography film, lay something on top of it, like a flower or leaves, then expose it to light. The picture you end up with depends on the amount of light and the kinds of chemicals you use when you process the film. It was pretty cool."

"It sounds like you had a creative chemistry teacher."

"She tried to make chemistry interesting. More than a bunch of formulas and equations, although we had to learn those, too. Projects like the photography prints were her way of showing us how chemistry affects our daily lives. That's what got me started in cooking. She showed us how chemistry is a big part of baking, and I was hooked."

"But what is this picture doing in Caro's gallery? It isn't like the other things she had there."

Becky took another look at the photo. "Not quite her style, is it?"

I copied the photo onto my laptop, then kept scrolling to the end of the file. Nothing stood out.

"Well, that was a waste of time," Becky said as she uncapped the purple marker. "Let's get started on this clue board."

"We don't have much, yet."

"Caro is the victim." Becky drew a square in the middle of the poster board and wrote Caro's name inside. "Who are the suspects?"

I tapped my chin with my finger as I considered. "There's Moose Morehead. Cal caught him leaving the gallery on Saturday morning."

Becky wrote down his name and drew a box around it. "Anyone else?"

"Right now, I would say Moose is the most likely, but it could have been anyone." I ran my fingers through my hair, frustrated. "We need to know more about Caro. Let's start making a list of what we learned last night." I pulled my Bullet Journal out of my bag and turned to a fresh page.

"Well, we know where she went to school," Becky started.

"That's a good place to start." I wrote down the name of the school. "And I'll add where she has taught at artist in residence programs." I opened up her website on my laptop.

"Is there a connection?"

"I have no idea. But yesterday I realized we don't know why Caro chose Paragon for her art colony. Why not Flagstaff? Or Tulsa? Or someplace in California?"

"You're right. Do you have a sticky note?"

"Great idea." I pulled a pad of square sticky notes out of my bag. "We'll write our speculations on sticky notes, and then we'll be able to get rid of them if we find out we're wrong. Hercule Poirot would be proud of us."

"Agatha Christie's detective?"

"Right." I reached for the book I had been reading and opened it to my bookmark. "He was talking to Colonel Race," I leafed back a few pages. "Here it is. He said some detectives won't throw out theories that don't match the evidence. Instead, they throw out evidence that doesn't match their theory." I put the book down. "We need to be sure we don't come up with an idea and then search for evidence that supports it."

"I get it. We need to follow the clues."

After I finished listing the artist in residence programs, I wrote down the few details we had gleaned from Caro's website and the date of her arrest.

"Now to the suspects." Becky held up the purple marker. "Should I start writing down names?"

"Not yet. Right now, everyone in town could be the murderer. With both locals and tourists, that's hundreds of people."

"Or thousands. Remember, we're in the middle of Paragon Days."

"That's right. Tomorrow is Memorial Day. There's a ceremony at the cemetery, right? Anything else?"

"And games for the kids at the park and a town-wide garage sale along Church Street. Main Street will be closed to traffic and all kinds of vendors will have booths and food trucks set up in the street. And then in the evening there will be an outdoor concert featuring local cowboy and western musicians." Becky capped her marker. "You should have taken the time to read the poster."

"You're right. I should do that. We have one at the reception desk."

Becky's phone pinged and she glanced at the screen.

"My cousin Maria says they need my help with the ice cream social. The crowd is bigger than they anticipated. I had better get down there."

"Ice cream social?"

Becky gave me her exasperated look. "You really need to read that poster. This evening is an old-fashioned ice cream social in the park, along with music from the Four Winds."

"Isn't that the Barbershop quartet your uncles have? They sang at church last week, didn't they?"

"Yup. That's them. Tonight, they'll be singing a variety of stuff like folk music and old songs from when they were younger. You know, Music Man kind of stuff. The crowd loves it. And Gran is in charge of the ice cream, but she can't do it on her own."

I felt a twinge of envy. "Your family pulls together to help Gran, don't they?"

She put the purple marker back in my bag. "When Gran calls, it's all hands on deck. But sometimes the calls come at inconvenient times."

"Don't worry about it. I think we're done here for now. We don't have enough information to go very far." I slid the crime board under the ottoman. "But your cousins might know something. You could get them started talking about Caro's death and see what comes up."

"You aren't thinking one of us is involved in her murder, are you?"

"No, of course not. But you never know what someone might have seen that connects with the investigation."

Becky grinned. "Now you're talking like one of those television mystery shows." She slid her phone into her purse and stood up, displacing Tim. "I'll see what I can do. And I'll see you at the social, right? You'll be there?"

I wasn't sure I wanted to spend my only free evening with a crowd of strangers, but the grin on Becky's face made my decision for me. "Yeah, I'll be there. Maybe I can pitch in and help with the ice cream."

"That would be great. You'll love it."

After she left, I made myself a cup of tea in my little kitchen. As it brewed, I looked through the crime scene photos again. When I got to the one of the framed print Caro had been holding, I enlarged it. The design of leaves was interesting, but very muted. Monochromatic. The other pieces of art in the gallery were bold. Either very colorful, like most of the paintings, or unique like Moose's metal sculptures. Caro had a style, and this print didn't fit. Where had it come from?

I sipped my tea as I went through the rest of the photos slowly, examining each one. Nothing else stood out as unusual. I closed the laptop and patted my lap, inviting Tim to snuggle. He ignored me, other than twitching the end of his tail, so I took my tea out to the balcony opening off my living room and leaned on the railing. I could barely make out the town of Paragon through the trees, but the traffic noises and other sounds that floated up the hill meant a lot of people were in town. Tourist season. The life blood of the inn and the other businesses in town, and Paragon Days was a great kick-off to the summer.

That thought reminded me I hadn't given the poster Becky had mentioned more than a glance. If any of our guests asked about the festival, I needed to know what was going on.

I headed downstairs to the reception desk where I had tacked the Paragon Days poster to the end of the counter. The margins of the poster were filled with ads from local businesses and in the center was the schedule of events. That evening, Sunday, the only thing scheduled was the old-fashioned ice cream social Becky had talked about. The next day, Memorial Day, was filled with activities all day, ending with the concert in the park.

The one event that wasn't going to happen was the show at the art gallery. Someone, probably Caro, had made sure the event was highlighted in bold print on the schedule. It looked like the art show had been one of the major attractions for the event. How many people would be coming to Paragon Days expressly for that?

Unpinning the poster from the front of the desk, I laid it on top of the desk and started reading the ads framing the schedule. Every business in Paragon had a square, starting with Gran's Café in the top center. I went clockwise around the poster, looking for the businesses I had visited with my brochures. The ads were placed in the same order you would find the businesses on Main Street. Each one had a logo or a picture and advertised a special deal for Paragon Days.

When I reached the ad for Living Wild, I stopped and leaned closer to look at the photo. Behind Anna Grace's smiling face was a display of monochromatic prints like the one in the crime scene photos. My fingers grew cold. Had Anna Grace given the print to Caro? Was she the one who had spread nicotine on the frame?

I jumped, startled, when Rose opened the door to her suite, her sun hat in one hand. Thatcher ran toward me.

"Emma! Are you feeling all right? You look like you've-"

"Seen a ghost?" I finished the question for her and forced myself to smile. "I was deep in thought, I guess. I forgot where I was." I bent down to pet the corgi before he could plant his forepaws on my knee. "It can't be time for Thatcher's walk already, can it?"

"It's nearly four o'clock." Rose frowned at me as she put her hat on. "Are you sure everything is okay?"

"This case has given me a lot to think about, and some of it isn't very pleasant." I chewed on my lower lip as I thought about how much to involve my aunt. "I could use your help deciding what to do about something I discovered."

Thatcher tugged Rose toward the front door. "We can talk after I get back from my walk. How many guests are coming back to the inn for tea?"

I found the list I kept on the desk. "Only Violet and Charles. No one else notified me they would be here. Do you think they forgot?"

"The Thomas family was going to be out all day sight-seeing, and they plan to be at Mount Rushmore for the evening ceremonies. The others are going to the ice cream social in Paragon." Rose followed Thatcher to the door. "Do you have everything set for Violet and Charles when they get here?"

"I will."

I waved as she went out the door and checked my phone. Ten 'til four. I had just enough time.

Under the buffet was a teapot that Rose used occasionally. Most guests liked to fix their tea by the cup, but if I had Viperish Violet and Charitable Charles pegged right, they would appreciate the extra touch. I spooned some of the French Creek Tea's bergamot blend into the diffuser and prepared the pot, complete with a tea cozy. I would fill it with hot water when they arrived.

In the kitchen I went to the freezer to grab a few scones to thaw in the microwave, but then had second thoughts. Becky's scones were delicious whether they were fresh or thawed from frozen, but why not go the extra mile this afternoon? Rose kept a supply of English tea biscuits on hand for her British friends Clara and Montgomery, and a package was still in the cupboard from their last visit. I went back to the buffet and found plates that matched the teapot. I lined the larger one with a paper doily, then arranged the biscuits on it.

Once I filled the tray with the teapot in its cozy, the matching cups, saucers, plates, and cream and sugar set, I stood back. The effect was charming and oh-so-British. I loved it and hoped Charles and Violet would, too.

I checked my phone again. Three minutes past four. And right on time, they came in the front door.

"It's so quiet. Are we the only ones here?" Violet's voice was loud enough to be heard in Becky's apartment.

"I'm here," I called back.

Charles wheeled Violet into the dining room. "We aren't too early for tea, are we?" he asked. "We've had a tiring day and would like to spend a quiet evening in our suite."

"Not at all. In fact, I just finished fixing your tray. Would you like your usual French Creek Grey, or would you like to try a different blend today?"

Violet gave a languid, dismissive wave with one hand. "The Grey is fine, I suppose. Bring it to our suite."

Charles wheeled her toward their door while I filled the pot with hot water from the urn. Violet seemed on edge this afternoon.

When I delivered the tray to their suite, Charles smiled his thanks, but Violet ignored me. She sat slumped in her wheelchair, facing away from the door. A twinge of pity reached my heart.

"Is she in much pain?" I asked Charles quietly as he saw me to the door.

"Pain?" Charles glanced over his shoulder at his wife before stepping out and closing the door behind him. "Yes, but not physical pain. The accident, you see, robbed her of everything that gave her joy in life. Her painting, her friends, her promising career. She has...times...when it becomes too much."

I smiled at him. "Those times are when she needs you the most."

Charles looked at the door, then back at me, his expression as opaque as a cloudy sky. "At those times, I'm not sure she even notices me."

He let himself back into the suite while I went back to the reception desk and the poster. But instead of studying the Living Wild ad again, I leaned my chin on my hand and stared at the closed door. The situation Charles described was sad. No wonder Violet was struggling.

Rose and Thatcher returned from their walk.

"Are Violet and Charles taken care of?" Rose asked.

"They're in their suite with a proper British tea."

My aunt smiled and broadened her native Cumbrian accent. "A proper British tea, then. Brilliant. Should we have ours in my suite? You can tell me what's bothering you."

I set up another tray and followed Rose to her comfortable living room, the poster tucked under my arm. Her suite occupied the front corner of the lower floor of the inn, directly below mine. The door of her office was closed, arousing my curiosity once again. Rose was keeping her memoirs secret from everyone, but I longed to read them. She had led an exciting life as an international spy before she came to the Black Hills and opened the inn. I still had trouble believing my sweet aunt had ever been a Jane Bond-type, but I had seen her keep her head in the most dangerous situations.

Rose poured tea for both of us, then took a tea biscuit for herself. She broke off a bit and gave it to Thatcher while I spread the poster on the coffee table in front of her sofa.

"Look at this ad for Living Wild," I said.

She leaned forward and studied it. "It's a good advertisement. Anna Grace has worked hard to get her store ready in time for this weekend and it shows. She has a good eye for design."

"When I found Caro's body, there was a picture in a frame lying face down on the floor next to her. Cal said the nicotine that killed her was on that frame."

Rose's eyes narrowed. "Ever since you told me the poison was nicotine, I've thought about how it was an excellent choice for the murderer. Many coroners wouldn't even think of it as a cause of death." She turned a questioning gaze toward me. "How is that connected to the ad?"

"Cal let Becky and I look at the crime scene photos. The picture with the nicotine on it is exactly like the ones here in Anna Grace's ad." I pointed to them. "But I can't believe Anna Grace is a murderer. She's so sweet."

Rose stirred cream into her tea. "I once knew a hired assassin who was a kind, loving grandmother in her other life. You can't take a person at face value when you're talking about murder." My face must have shown my shock. "But don't worry. Not every murderer is able to hide their true nature as well as she was."

"But what do I do? Do I confront Anna Grace?"

"With what? You have no evidence other than the coincidental appearance of a picture similar to ones Anna Grace sells." Rose took a sip of her tea, then set the cup back in its saucer with a steady clink. "Has Cal determined Caro was murdered?"

"He still thinks her death could be accidental. The

amount of nicotine wasn't lethal for most people."

"Then why does the coroner say it was the cause of her death?"

"She had a heart condition, so a smaller dose was enough to kill her."

Rose patted the couch next to her and Thatcher jumped up. He laid his head in her lap and she rubbed his ears, a thoughtful expression on her face. I nibbled on a tea biscuit while I waited.

"I lean toward murder," she finally said.

"You think the murderer knew about Caro's heart condition?"

"Not necessarily. It could have been someone who didn't know how to determine the lethal dose. Most poisoners will make sure their poison works by administering much more than a lethal dose. But in this case, it wasn't that strong." She picked up her teacup again. "Either the murderer knew Caro well enough to know about her health problems, or he isn't very good at what he does."

"That means it could be anyone," I said, but my thoughts went to Moose Morehead. He didn't seem like the type who would be concerned with the finer details of poisons.

"Not anyone. It was someone. But you're right, the field of suspects is a broad one, so you need to start narrowing it. Meanwhile, you could ask Anna Grace about the picture. How many of them has she sold? And to whom?"

"But if she's the murderer, wouldn't that clue her in to our suspicions?"

Rose smiled. "You're talented enough to get the information without letting her know exactly what you're looking for." She patted my knee. "Just get her to talk about the pictures, and she might tell you exactly what you need to know."

"I'll head down there tomorrow morning. I should be able to stop in after breakfast and before the town gets too busy." I drank the last of my tea and picked up another biscuit. "Meanwhile, I'm heading down to the ice cream social. I told Becky I'd help out."

"Have fun." Rose shooed me away when I started to pick up our tea tray. "I'll take care of this. You go on into town and do some sleuthing."

Seven

Since my arrival in Paragon at the end of April, the city park had been a beautiful green space. A peaceful and quiet spot across from the church at the foot of the hills.

But tonight? Café lights were strung from poles around the perimeter of the park, glowing in the early evening twilight. The effect gave the area the look of a carnival. Tourists walked in groups, a few picking wisps of cotton candy from the cloud in their hand, others clutching a stuffed toy animal they had won at the ring toss game. In my quest to find the ice cream booth, I passed one young father carrying a bear as big as the toddler walking beside him.

Balloons floated in the air right at eye-level, obscuring my vision. Where was Gran's booth? I spied someone licking an ice cream cone, then another. I followed the trail to its source - a food trailer with Gran's Café painted on the side. I picked my way through the boxes and power cords at the end of the truck and knocked on the door.

"Hey." A disheveled Becky swung the door open. "If you're here to help, I sure need you."

I climbed into the workspace and tied on the

apron she tossed to me. "Where are all your cousins?"

"We're spread too thin." She scooped chocolate ice cream into a cone and handed it to the customer at the outside counter. "Cheyenne and Stephanie decided to open a face painting booth, and Cal is working at the ring toss along with the boys. The rest of the guys are either still setting up or directing traffic." She gave the customer his change and glanced at me, pushing her hair out of her face with the back of her wrist. "Thanks for coming."

"What do I do?"

"Grab an ice cream scoop. The first scoop is free, then you charge them if they want more."

I slipped on a pair of gloves as I watched Becky serve the next customer. It looked easy enough. I turned to the next person in line.

"What would you like?"

"Chocolate, please."

I scraped the scoop along the sides of the chocolate ice cream in the counter freezer and handed the cone to her. Then on to the next customer. I looked beyond that person and sighed. The line was six people deep and getting longer by the second.

An hour later, the crowd began to thin out. Becky had switched an empty vanilla tub for a fresh one from the cooler truck in the back and as she let the three-gallon tub drop into the freezer she grinned at me.

"Having fun?"

I stretched my arms, loosening the kinks that had developed. "You know I am."

Another customer walked up, and my smile faded. Moose Morehead.

"Can I get some ice cream?" he asked.

I gave myself a mental shake. He was just another customer. "Sure. What kind?"

"You got any butter pecan?"

Pointing to the sign tacked on the outside of the truck, I said, "We have vanilla and chocolate."

"Give me three scoops of vanilla."

I grabbed a cone and reached for a scoop. "That will be a dollar."

He leaned against the counter. "I thought the ice cream was free."

"The first scoop is free. If you want more, it's fifty cents a scoop."

I ignored his growl and started filling his cone. While I worked, someone else came up to the truck.

"Hey, Moose. I heard you were in jail."

"They couldn't hold me. Not enough evidence."

I fumbled the second scoop and it fell back into the freezer. Not enough evidence? Cal had caught him red-handed with the drugs. But then, I guess Moose could have claimed he didn't know the package was at the bottom of the box.

"What about the art show? Is it still going on?"

"Naw. With Caro dead and the gallery closed, there's no place to hold it."

"Too bad. I was hoping to pick up some pieces for my bar."

I started on Moose's third scoop.

"I could show you what I've got. We could work out a deal. You know my stuff would sell great in Sturgis."

"Better than in this backwater."

I bristled at the man's slam on my new hometown.

"You're talking about selling it in my bar?" The man continued the conversation as I handed Moose his ice cream and took his money. "On commission?"

"Yeah. I could keep you supplied, and we can split the profits."

The man drummed his fingers on the counter while Moose took a bite out of his ice cream. "I'll think about it. Where's your stuff?"

"In my car." Moose thumbed in the direction of Main Street. "I'll show you."

I watched them walk away as I fingered the dollar bill Moose had handed me. I had assumed the two men had been talking about Moose's sculptures, but had that really been the subject of their conversation? I could believe Moose had been making a deal for selling drugs from the guy's bar in Sturgis.

"What's up?" Becky asked. "You look like you're pondering a deep question."

"I overheard a conversation-" I dropped the thought and laughed. "I think I might be trying too hard to solve this murder."

"What murder?"

I hadn't seen the next customer walk up to the counter. It was a man wearing a tee shirt from Yellowstone with a picture of Old Faithful.

"Sorry." I grabbed a clean ice cream scoop. "It's in a book I'm reading. I'm really caught up in it."

"Yeah. Well. I guess some people do that." He pointed to the sign. "I'll take chocolate."

A few members of the group that had been outside the art gallery yesterday morning walked up.

"I tell you, it isn't like Caro to suddenly drop over dead like that," said a thin man with a long gray braid. "There's something fishy going on."

Thankfully, the Yellowstone tourist had already walked away.

"Well," said a young woman wearing a hot pink sweatsuit, "I think what's fishy is that no one has seen Caro, and the police aren't talking. I don't think she's dead at all, but only pretending to be."

"Why would she do that?" asked a twenty-something man in a black tee shirt.

"To take off with our entry fees. Do you think we'll ever see our money again? Caro Lewis will change her name and play the same scam in some other town."

"I heard she was murdered." The man with the braid glanced at the sign on the trailer. "Chocolate."

I started scooping.

The guy with the black tee shirt took a step away from the others. "I don't want to have anything to do with murder."

Pink sweatsuit narrowed her eyes as she watched his reaction. "If I was investigating this crime, you'd be at the top of my suspect list."

"Why me?" His splayed hands showed white against his black shirt. "I didn't even know her."

"You don't have to know someone to kill them. You probably stole the money, too." She put her fists on her hips and sneered at him. "Where's the cash, Chuck? Or did you already blow through it?"

"Is everything all right here?"

I had never been so glad to see Cal. His hands were on his utility belt as he approached the group.

"Oh, geez, the cops." Black tee shirt melted into the shadows between the food truck and the face painting booth.

"Everything is fine." The man with the braid took his chocolate cone and put an arm around pink sweatsuit's shoulder. "We're only having a friendly conversation."

The girl gave a nervous giggle. "Can I have a vanilla cone?"

"Sure." I scooped it into a cone for her and the pair walked away.

"You two all right?" Cal asked.

"We're fine," Becky answered. "But you came along just in time. Those three were about to come to blows."

"Yeah. I heard that." Cal rubbed the back of his neck. "That art crowd is getting pretty testy. With the show being canceled, they're out a lot of money."

"And it sounds like they have a lot of questions."

I chewed on my bottom lip. Should I tell Cal about Moose and his deal? But before I could say anything, Pete Clarkson, the owner of Pete's Sammiches came up. I had met him and his brother when I had dropped brochures off at their shop the other day.

"Have you seen my brother Mike around?" He ran his hand through his hair, doing no favors to his already disheveled look. "He was going to come over here to get a couple ice cream cones for the two of us, but then he never came back to the restaurant."

"What time was that?" Cal asked.

"Right when the ice cream social opened, at six o'clock."

The deputy looked at his watch. "Two hours ago. Could he have gone someplace else?"

Pete shook his head. "I already checked with Anna Grace, but he hadn't stopped to see her. Mike has some problems with his memory. He has trisomy 21. Down's syndrome. He's pretty capable in spite of his disability, but we're partners. He would never leave me to handle the evening crowd on my own, not if he could help it." He ran his hand through his hair again. "Him not doing what he promised...he takes stuff like that seriously. I'm pretty worried about him."

"I'll take a look around," Cal said.

"What if you don't find him?" Pete said. "I don't know what I'd do if something happened to him."

"We don't know anything bad has happened. Don't worry. We'll find out what delayed him."

"It's time for us to close," Becky said. "We can help you look."

Cal met my eyes with a nod. "I'd appreciate it."

Cal and Pete started around the circle of booths at the social while Becky and I closed the food truck. We locked the back door, and I started toward the outer edges of the lit area.

"Where are you going?" Becky whispered as she caught up to me.

"I thought we'd look behind the booths." I remembered how black tee shirt guy had melted into the darkness once he got out of the circle of the café lights. Anything or anyone could be hidden in the gloom.

"We won't be able to see anything back here."

"It isn't full-on dark, yet. Once our eyes get used to it, we'll be able to see. Let's head toward Clear Creek Road, and then circle back around."

I stopped once we got to the back of the cooler truck to let my eyes adjust.

"You think something happened to him?" Becky asked.

"I don't know. But we have to look."

We walked in the twilight behind the booths. We surprised a couple in the middle of a passionate kiss behind the ring-toss booth. Becky hurried past them.

"My cousin, Stephanie," she said in a whisper. "Gran doesn't like her boyfriend."

"They're sneaking around behind her back? That can't be good."

"Nothing good ever comes from trying to hide something from Gran. I'll talk to Stephanie tomorrow."

When we circled toward the far side of the park, the church loomed against the dark blue sky. Even this late, the remains of this evening's sunset lingered at the edges of the hills above the town.

"Let's walk through the cemetery."

Becky grabbed my arm. "The cemetery? In the dark? No way."

"The biggest danger is you'll stub your toe on a grave marker."

"We should have brought a flashlight."

"We have our cell phones if we need them. But there's enough light to see where we're walking. We'll be fine."

Becky grabbed my arm and hung on as we walked along the edge of the cemetery. The park was quieting down now that the booths were closed, and people were straggling to their cars.

Ahead of us was a black form on the ground.

"It looks like someone threw out their trash bag," Becky said. "I don't know why they don't use the trash cans in the park."

She let go of my arm and walked over to the black lump. She reached down to pick it up but jumped back.

"What's wrong?"

"It isn't a trash bag. It's a person."

My heart dropped into my shoes as I grabbed my

phone and turned on the flashlight app. The form was too sprawled out. Too still. I shined the light on the face.

"No, it can't be."

Becky looked at me, her face white in the glow of the lights in the park. "Is it Mike?"

I nodded. "I'm going to call Cal."

Cal was on the scene in minutes. Along with Pete.

"You found him?"

"Pete, he's -" I looked to Cal for help.

"Let me check him first. Give me a minute." Cal pushed past us and went to Mike's still form.

I tried to hold Pete back, but he tore away from me and dropped to his knees next to his brother.

"Mike!" He put his hand on the still form, then sat back on his heels. "He can't be gone. He can't be."

The despair in Pete's voice caused a painful twist in my stomach. Cal was on his phone calling for the EMTs, so I put my arms around Pete's shoulders and tried to draw him away.

"You need to let Cal do his work. The ambulance is on its way."

Cal nodded his thanks for my help, then started his examination. Becky took Pete's other arm and we both stood with him as we waited.

"He's actually gone, isn't he?" Pete shuddered. "What am I going to do without him? He's my brother. The only family I have."

"I'm sorry," I said. I rubbed his back, but I couldn't comfort him.

Pete clung to Becky. "He had a check-up last

month, and the doctor said he was doing okay."

Cal drove his SUV over to the scene and shined his spotlight on the cemetery. The crowds at the ice cream social were dwindling, but those who were left noticed something unusual going on and drifted toward us. Among them was Rose. When she saw us standing off to the side she came over, Thatcher straining at his leash.

"Emma, what happened?"

I bent over to pet Thatcher. The corgi ignored me and sat at our feet, watching Mike's body.

I gave Rose the short version of the evening, ending with, "and then we found Mike here."

My aunt's face was stony. "Do we know how he died?"

"Not yet."

Cal finished his examination, then retrieved a blanket from his SUV and spread it over Mike. One hand extended beyond the blanket's cover and before Cal could adjust it, Thatcher approached, sniffing delicately. He barely touched the splayed fingers, then backed away with a whine. The dog crouched a foot away and looked at me. The whites of his eyes gleamed in the artificial light. He whined again.

I looked from Thatcher to Mike's hand as Cal pulled the edge of the blanket over it. Was my canine buddy trying to tell me something?

Cal's voice was gentle as he spoke to Pete. "It looks like a heart attack, but we'll know more when we get him back to the lab."

Pete strained to see past Cal's bulk to his brother's body on the ground. He ran his hand over his face. "An autopsy? Is it necessary?"

"I'm afraid so. It's an unattended death."

"But he's my little brother. I'm supposed to watch out for him."

Anna Grace pushed through the circle of watching people and took Becky's place next to Pete.

"I heard what happened. Pete, I'm sorry."

She put her arm around him, and he turned to her, gathering her in close.

Sirens sounded in the distance and Rose took charge.

"I think it's time to let the medical team take care of Mike."

"That's right," Cal said, giving Rose a relieved glance. "You'll all be able to visit the bod-" He cleared his throat. "Mike will be at the coroner's office in Rapid City, and you'll be able to visit him there tomorrow. I'll let you know."

"Let's go up to the inn for some tea." Rose gave Thatcher's leash to me as she started moving Pete and Anna Grace in that direction. "You shouldn't be alone at this time, and I know you don't want to go home right now."

As they started toward the inn, I stayed behind with Becky.

"A heart attack?" I asked Cal. "Don't you think that's a little suspicious?"

"Suspicious? Why?" He took a toothpick from his pocket and stuck it in the corner of his mouth.

"That's the same cause of death as Caro. Don't you think it's too much of a coincidence?"

He gave me his stony deputy look. "Two people having a heart attack isn't suspicious. People do die from natural causes sometimes."

"Something feels hinky to me."

"Emma's right," Becky said. "We could have two

murders on our hands."

Cal glanced at the crowd, but their attention was on the ambulance as they gave it room to come into the cemetery.

"Keep your voices down, and don't mention that word. We don't know if there's any connection between the two deaths yet. You need to let me do my job."

"Let's go," I said. "Cal has things under control here, and we'll learn more in the morning."

I tugged both Becky and Thatcher away from the scene and started walking back to the inn.

"But we could get more information from Cal," Becky said as she followed me.

"At this point, I think we might be able to learn more from Pete."

Becky quickened her pace. "You're right. Let's get up there before Rose starts interrogating him."

I would have laughed at her reaction if the situation hadn't been so grim.

"Interrogating isn't what I would call it."

We crossed the highway and started up Graves' Gulch Road.

"Interviewing? Questioning?"

I linked elbows with her. "Comforting. Rose is very good at making people feel comfortable in all situations. I can see her now, calmly sitting at one of the dining room tables, serving a cup of herbal tea to Pete."

But when we got to the inn, the quiet peace I had envisioned wasn't anywhere to be seen. I had been right about the herbal tea, but Pete was surrounded by our concerned guests. I took one look and started replenishing the tea supplies.

Anna Grace was next to Pete while the Brooks sisters, Dave and Joy Albert, and Rick and Debbie Walker sat at the next table, listening. Violet was on the other side of Pete from Rose, with Charles sitting next to her.

"I'm sorry this has happened, Pete," Rose was saying. "Mike was a special ray of sunshine in Paragon, and he'll be missed."

Pete sniffed. "Thanks." He stared at his cup. "I shouldn't have let him go to the social alone, but he really likes ice cream."

"It isn't your fault." Rose said. "The deputy said his death was from natural causes, didn't he?"

"But if I had kept him at the sandwich shop-" His voice broke.

Violet made a sudden move, as if she was trying to reach out to comfort Pete.

Anna Grace rubbed his arm. "It could have happened anywhere, at any time. It could have happened while he was helping me out at Living Wild this afternoon."

"Did he have any medical issues?" Violet asked.

"Mike was born with a heart condition, but he's outlived all the doctors' predictions by ten years." He hiccupped. "I guess - I guess I thought those doctors must be wrong, even though the septum defect was still there. I can't believe he's gone."

Betty Ann clucked her tongue and Sally Marie dabbed at her eyes with a handkerchief.

"That poor man," she said. "I would never get over losing you, dear sister."

Pete stared at the cup in front of him. He didn't seem to notice anyone else was around.

The Thomas family came in talking about their

experience at Mt. Rushmore and Pete cringed. Terri faltered when she saw the group in the dining room.

"Is something wrong? What has happened?"

Rose whispered something to Anna Grace, then the two of them ushered Pete into Rose's suite. I headed the Thomas family off at the reception desk.

"I'm sorry. Pete lost his brother tonight."

"Is that why we saw the ambulance in Paragon?" Ted asked. "I wondered if someone had gotten hurt."

"Yes, the ambulance was there. I'm glad you missed it." I smiled and changed the subject as I turned to the girls. "Tell me all about your evening at Mt. Rushmore. What did you see?"

Toni twirled around. "You should have been there. Dad went up on the stage with a bunch of other people. It was so cool!"

"It was pretty awesome," Taylor said. "Dad's a veteran and they made a big deal about it."

Terri linked her arm in Ted's. "I'm glad they did. Your dad gave a lot for his country."

"It was ages ago," Toni said. "Before I was born."

"I remember, though." Taylor took her dad's other arm. "I remember when you came home from the war. You had been gone forever."

Ted put his arms around his wife and daughter. "It seems like yesterday to me. But the ceremony was great. It brought back a lot of good memories, like that day I came home and was able to be with my family again."

"Well, girls, we should go upstairs." Terri guided Toni toward the stairs. "You can have fifteen minutes of screen time, then it's off to bed."

While the rest of the family went up to their rooms, Taylor hung back.

"This guy who died, what happened to him?"

"It looks like he had a heart attack."

"Oh."

"You sound disappointed."

Taylor sighed. "I was hoping he had been killed suspiciously and I could help solve the mystery."

I smiled. "A girl after my own heart. Between reading murder mysteries and watching police dramas on television, I see a murder to solve in every unexplained death."

Her dark eyes shone. "That's it. You get it." She glanced up the stairs. "Mom said you really did solve a murder, just last month."

"Three, actually. I didn't do it by myself. A team of us worked together and figured out what was going on. The bad guy was caught and taken care of."

"But that doesn't mean there won't be another murder to solve, does it?"

I thought of the events of the past couple days. "There's always that possibility."

We said good night, and I went into the kitchen where Becky was prepping for the next morning.

"It's been a busy day," I said as I leaned against the counter.

Becky put a cover over a big bowl of bread dough. "And tomorrow will be even busier, with all the activities in town. And at ten o'clock there is the Memorial Day service at the cemetery."

I shuddered a little, thinking of finding Mike there a couple hours before. "Are you going?"

"Of course, I am. My dad is one of the veterans buried there and I go every year to honor his memory."

"I didn't know that. When did he serve?"

"He was in Vietnam in the 1970s." She wiped off the prep counter, her movements slower than normal. "He never recovered from his experience there and eventually died of multiple myeloma. They think it might have been caused by exposure to Agent Orange."

"I'm sorry, Becks."

"Thanks. What I miss most is that I never got to know him. I was only three when he died, and the only memory I have of him is pretty fuzzy." She finished wiping off the counter and rinsed her towel in the sink. "But that doesn't keep me from honoring him every Memorial Day."

"I'd like to join you for the ceremony."

She gave me one of her quick hugs. "That would be great. See you in the morning."

On the way up to my room, I thought through the evening. The biggest question I had was why Mike died when he did. Sure, with his poor health, he could have had a heart attack at any time, but why tonight? He had been fine earlier in the day, according to both Anna Grace and Pete.

Wait. What had Anna Grace said? Mike had been with her at her store in the afternoon. Could there be two deaths connected to Living Wild?

I ran the rest of the way to my room. The morning would bring more information and opportunities to get to the bottom of these two deaths. I only hoped we weren't dealing with another killer.

Eight

The aroma of fresh baked bread hit me before I started down the stairs on Monday morning. Bringing Becky to the Sweetbrier Inn was more evidence of Rose's genius. It gave Becky more room to work her baking magic than she had in the kitchen at Gran's Café, and she was surprisingly creative as she developed new breakfast ideas for the guests. And who could resist the yeasty fragrance of bread baking early each morning?

I started the coffee in the dining room, then went into the kitchen. Becky was at the prep counter working with some berries and thick triangles of French toast.

"What are you doing?" I asked as I poured myself a cup of coffee from the kitchen coffee maker.

"Making sure I can get this breakfast to look right."

She stood the triangles of French toast on their sides, the points rising above the plate like mountain peaks. Then she drizzled a white glaze over the toast, spilled raspberries and blueberries between and on top of the toast slices, and for a final touch, she gave everything a dusting of powdered sugar.

She stood back. "What do you think?"

"It's beautiful. Very patriotic and a feast for the eyes. I love it."

"I thought we should have something special for Memorial Day." She turned the plate to inspect it from all sides, then got two forks from a drawer. "We need to do a final test, though."

She handed a fork to me, and I cut a portion of the toast off, making sure to get a couple berries, too. I popped it into my mouth.

"Um." I nodded to her as she took her own taste. "Um. Delicious. Perfect. Keep this recipe." I took another bite. "Did I taste cream cheese in the glaze?"

"That bit of a tang is a perfect complement to the sweetness of the fruit, don't you think?"

The oven timer dinged. Becky took two pans of hamburger buns out of the oven and set them on the end of the prep counter before she slid two more pans out of her proofing rack and put them in. She set the timer then turned back to me.

"Are you planning to go into town today?"

"I'm going to the ceremony at the cemetery with you, but before that I thought I'd drop in on Anna Grace. She sells pictures like the one at the crime scene."

"You don't think Anna Grace is involved in Caro's death, do you?"

I picked up another raspberry. "You know what Cal says." I popped the fruit into my mouth.

"Everyone is a suspect." Becky picked up a spatula and started moving the hamburger buns from the baking tray to a cooling rack.

"But I want to know what Mike did yesterday, and Anna Grace said he had spent some time helping her in her shop. Maybe she noticed something unusual about him. Do you want to come with me?"

"I have to start another batch of bread. Gran's is getting busier every day, and I don't want the café to run out of buns.

Breakfast was a success. The guests loved the Patriotic French Toast and sausage links. The conversations in the dining room didn't dwell on last night's death like I thought they might. Rose had started the conversation on a safe subject by asking everyone what their plans were for the day.

"We're shopping in town," Sally Marie said. "We love street fairs, don't we Betty Ann?"

"And I want to buy a souvenir from one of the stores." Her sister giggled. "I buy something special from every trip we take."

"Did I see something about a Memorial Day ceremony?" Ted asked. He was at the breakfast bar, helping himself to more sausage links.

"It's at the cemetery at ten o'clock," Rose said.

Dave and Joy had been conferring with Rick and Debbie. "We both want to visit Devils Tower, so we'll be heading to Wyoming for the day."

Only Violet and Charles remained silent. Violet looked uncomfortable in her chair, and I thought perhaps she was still tired from the day before. Charles leaned over to say something to her. She shook her head and pointed toward the door of their suite. It looked like the elderly couple was going to stay in.

At nine o'clock I stuck my head in the kitchen. Becky was mixing dough in her big stand mixer.

"I'm on my way out. See you at the cemetery?"

"I'll be there right before ten."

I gave her a thumbs-up and headed toward Paragon.

The town was busy. Main Street was blocked off and street vendors were setting up tables and canopies. I nodded to a few friendly faces as I walked down the center of the street. It looked like there was a lot a variety in the offerings, everything from antiques to doll clothes to books by local authors. Living Wild was still closed when I reached the front door, but Anna Grace saw me through the window and let me in.

"How are you this morning?"

Anna Grace's eyes were red. "I couldn't sleep last night. Pete went home, but I worried about him all night. I know how hard it is to be alone after a loved one's death."

"Does he live in town?"

"He has an apartment on the second floor of his building like I do." She pointed to the stairway at the rear of her store.

"You said Mike spent some time with you yesterday afternoon, right? How did he seem?"

Anna Grace pulled out a tissue and dabbed her eyes. "He was such a great guy. He came over and said he wanted to help out here since Pete didn't need him between lunch and supper. I gave him the feather duster." She sniffed. "He had so much fun with it, humming a tune and dancing between the displays."

"Dancing?"

"Oh, maybe not dancing, but you know. Like this." She did a couple steps, then turned to the right and repeated the steps. "Nothing fancy, just fun. The customers enjoyed it."

I was beginning to regret not having the time to

know Mike better.

"He was feeling pretty good, then? He wasn't tired or stressed or anything?"

"Not at all. He was here for an hour or so and dusted the whole place. I appreciated it so much, I gave him one of the pictures he liked."

"Pictures?"

"Yes. One of these."

She led me to a display of photographic prints, very similar to the one Caro had been holding when she died.

"I wrapped up the one he chose. He said it was going to be a surprise for Pete. I thought it was very sweet of him."

"The brothers were close, weren't they?"

She dabbed at her eyes again. "They were. Mike's death has hit Pete hard." She checked her watch. "If you'll excuse me, I have a couple things to do before I open the store at ten."

I looked at my phone display. Nine-fifty-five. No time to ask about how many of those pictures she had sold. "I've got to get going. Thanks for talking with me."

When I reached the edge of the cemetery, I met Becky and Rose with Thatcher on his leash. At the base of the flagpoles in the center was a paved area where people were gathered, including the Thomas family. Becky had joined Gran and her family while Rose and I stood at the edge of the crowd. Behind us was an area everyone avoided, the place where Becky and I had found Mike's body. Crime scene tape fluttered in the breeze.

We all listened while Becky's Uncle Ben read the Declaration of Independence and Pastor Charlie read the names of the veterans who were buried in Paragon, some dating back to the Civil War. The ceremony ended with a three-gun salute.

As the crowd dispersed, Cal made his way over to me.

"I got the coroner's preliminary report this morning."

"On a holiday?"

He gave me one of his looks. "The police force doesn't take holidays off." He looked around at the groups wandering through the cemetery, reading the inscriptions on the stones. Gran was placing flowers on several of the graves.

"What did the coroner say?"

"The routine tox screen showed nicotine. Not enough to kill him, especially a man of his size, but enough to cause his heart to give out."

"You're saying if Mike hadn't had a heart condition, he wouldn't have died?"

Cal nodded. "The same as Caro. Without that, they probably would have noticed their heart racing or palpitations, but it wouldn't have affected them as severely."

"Are you thinking this might be a prank gone wrong?"

"I don't know what to think at this point. Two people are dead, prank or not."

Rose joined in. "Or the killer is good at estimating the correct dosage of the poison."

"You know about poisons?" Cal asked.

"I know something of them. And nicotine is one that is difficult to target the dose, unless you know your intended victim very well."

Cal stuck a toothpick in the corner of his mouth.

"What do you mean?"

"You need to know your victim's weight, but also any health history that might influence the effectiveness of the drug."

"Like a heart problem?"

"Exactly. It would take a smaller dosage to kill someone with Caro's condition than a healthy woman her same size."

"I need to talk with Pete about his brother." The toothpick shifted to the other corner of his mouth. "Do you want to come along?"

"I must get back to the inn and my writing. I'll leave the legwork to you two." Rose patted her leg and Thatcher followed her.

Cal frowned.

"What's wrong?"

"Just when I think I know Rose pretty well, she surprises me."

"You mean her knowledge of nicotine as a poison?"

"Yup." Cal turned toward his SUV and I fell into step beside him. "If I didn't know she had worked for the WIO, I'd wonder if she was planning a few murders herself."

I climbed into the passenger seat. "At least she's on our side. Her days with the World Intelligence Organization taught her a lot of things, but she's not a bad guy."

Cal drove down the alley between Main and Church Streets until he reached Pete's Sammiches. He parked, then we went up the outside stairway to the second floor of the building. Cal rapped his knuckles on the door.

When Pete opened it, I almost didn't recognize him. The dark shadow of his unshaved beard combined with his reddened eyes gave him a spectral look.

He glanced at us and opened the door further as he took a step back. "C'mon in."

As I entered, I tried not to let my gaze linger on the empty whiskey bottle on the floor and the nearly empty one on the table next to a recliner. Pete followed us in. He swept up some papers from the couch to give us a place to sit, then stood in the center of the floor looking around until he finally stashed them behind the chair.

"How are you doing, Pete?" Cal asked as we sat on the couch.

Pete slumped into the recliner. He ran one hand down his face. "Not so good."

"You've been drinking?"

"Wouldn't you?" Pete glared at Cal.

"Hey, I'm not judging," Cal said as he took a notepad and pen out of his pocket. "I was hoping we could ask you a few questions about Mike."

"Why?"

"It's only routine." Cal clicked his pen. "Was Mike acting normally yesterday?"

"Yeah." Pete ran both hands through his hair, started reaching for the glass of whiskey next to him, then pulled his hand back, leaving the glass where it was. "Yeah. He was happy, but he always was when he had a goal. He likes-" He scratched his whiskers. "He liked Anna Grace, next door. He was excited about spending some time in her shop."

"Was his excitement unusual?"

Pete shook his head. "Nope. Just pure Mike."

"What time did he get home?"

"He got to the shop around four o'clock, in time for the supper crowd. But he must have come up here first."

Cal made a couple notes. "Why do you say that?"

"I could tell he had been here. He had a habit of getting himself a glass of milk and forgetting to put the jug back in the fridge. The gallon was sitting on the table when I came upstairs after the supper rush." Pete squeezed his eyes shut. "I don't know how many times I yelled at him about it."

"When did he go to get the ice cream?"

"As soon as the social opened at six." He reached for the glass again but didn't take a drink. He cradled it in his hands. "He wanted to get two cones, one for each of us. I told him to go and come back quick because customers were coming in the door." He drained the last few drops remaining in the glass and glanced at the bottle. "I didn't know it would the last time I would ever talk to him." He looked at Cal. "When can I see my brother?"

"I'll take you. Get yourself showered and dressed. We'll leave as soon as you're ready."

"I'll put a sign on the door for you so your customers know you'll be closed today," I said as I stood up. "Then I need to get back to the inn."

I gave Cal a smile I could feel wobbling as I let myself out the door.

By the time I had posted the notice and walked back to the Sweetbrier, the wobble had turned into tears. What was wrong with me?

I was able to avoid talking to anyone at the inn by going through the garage, up the stairs to Becky's apartment, then through the second-floor lounge and into my suite. I threw myself onto my bed. Some unnamed emotion washed over me, threatening to drown me. I groaned and turned over. What was wrong with me?

I pulled my pillow over my eyes. If I could, I'd never face the world again. I began to recognize the emotion. I had felt the same way when I had realized Bruce had been lying to me. I threw the pillow to the side. Why didn't I push Cal to find Caro's killer before he struck again?

Tim came to investigate. He had never seen me like this before. I propped myself up on my pillows and pulled him into my arms. He pushed his head under my chin and purred.

"How did I ever survive without you, buddy?" I asked. In my years of working in various resorts around the world, I had never been allowed the luxury of a cat, but I appreciated the fuzz therapy he gave me now.

I stroked his fur, feeling myself relax, and tried to get a handle on that anger I had felt - was still feeling.

It was Mike. His death was so senseless. So cruel. What if he had been the victim of a murderer, too?

A knock sounded on my door. "Emma?" It was Rose's voice. "Are you all right?"

I tucked Tim under my arm and went to let Rose in.

She took one look at me, then walked into my kitchenette and put the kettle on. "You look like you need to talk. I'll make some tea."

As she rummaged in my cupboards for the tea service she had given me a few weeks ago to celebrate our partnership in the Sweetbrier, I sat on the couch, still petting Tim. Before the kettle boiled, he had had enough cuddling and jumped onto the back of the couch.

While I waited for Rose, I thought about Mike. Again, I wished I had gotten to know him better. Both Pete and Anna Grace had been devastated by their loss. How many other lives had Mike impacted?

Rose set the tea tray on the ottoman. "I chose the French Creek Tidbit. It's your favorite, isn't it?"

She was right. I loved the vanilla and almond flavored blend of black and green teas. "How could you tell?"

"I used the last of it for this pot." She laced her fingers around one knee. "Now, can you tell me what's wrong?"

I slumped against the back of the couch. "What tipped you off?"

"I saw your face as you came charging up the driveway earlier. Something upset you."

I fingered the hem of my cardigan. I could never hide anything from Rose.

"I don't know why, but Mike's death has devastated me."

She nodded. "It was senseless. If we were sure he had died of natural causes, it would be a sad tragedy."

"That's just it. After Caro's death, I didn't consider the killer might strike again, but I should have." I watched as Rose poured tea for both of us. "I can't help feeling it's my fault that Mike is dead."

Rose stirred some sugar into her tea before adding a bit of milk. Using the little pitcher that was part of the tea set rather than pouring directly out of the quart I kept in my mini fridge was one of the reasons I loved Rose. Little details like that mattered to her.

She took a sip of her tea, then looked at me as she set her cup back on its saucer. "Mike's death is not your fault."

"But if I could have prevented it-"

Rose shook her head. "You can't think that way. We can't see everything, and we can't be everywhere. Even if Mike was murdered, you had no way to predict he was going to be the next victim."

I sipped my own tea. The vanilla and almond flavors washed through me, soothing my anger a bit, but not that unnamed feeling of... I set my cup down harder than I had intended, and it clashed against the saucer. Shame. That's what it was. I was ashamed.

"I need to quit pursuing murderers every time someone dies around here."

"Why?"

Tim had walked to Rose across the back of the sectional, and she gathered him into her lap.

"I'm no good at this." I sat up, leaning toward her. "Look at what happened last month. You were nearly killed. Twice. If I hadn't gotten involved, none of that would have happened. I'm no detective." I leaned back again, defeated. "I need to leave crime solving to the professionals."

Rose scratched Tim under the chin, making him purr. "I disagree. If it hadn't been for your detective work, that case may never have been solved. And more people might have died, including me. And you."

"But look at all the mistakes I made. I accused the wrong person then and nearly let the killer get away." I picked up my cup of tea again. "And now I'm trying to make Caro's death into a murder. What if it isn't? What if both Caro's and Mike's deaths were really from natural causes and I'm wasting both my time and Cal's looking for a connection that doesn't exist?"

Rose's voice was quiet. "Do you truly believe that?"

"No." I had to admit that much. "But what if I'm wrong?"

"What if you're right?"

I thought about her question as I finished my tea. She poured another cup for both of us.

"This desire you have to solve crimes is a good one. Protecting people and bringing criminals to justice is the legacy of the Blackwoods. It's in your blood."

"Dad never thought it was."

"He told you Harry and I were wasting our lives, didn't he?"

I nodded. "Especially after Uncle Harry died."

"Your uncle's death affected your father greatly. But earlier, before your mother passed away, your father was invaluable to Harry's work."

"Dad? How?"

"Harry would fly to the States whenever he could to consult with your father. Harry always said George was as good of an armchair detective as Mycroft Holmes."

"Sherlock's brother?"

"Your father had an instinct for solving crimes, and Harry relied on his insights. You have that same instinct."

"Then what happened? I only remember Dad hating what Harry did. I can't imagine him the way you describe him."

Rose sighed as her eyes took on a distant look. "Your mother's death. He couldn't have prevented it.

It was cancer that cut her life short, not an evil force, but he still felt responsible. He told Harry not to involve him in our work anymore, and he concentrated his energy on you." She laid her hand on my knee. "He loved you very much, you know."

I took her hand in mine. "I wish I could have known Dad the way you describe him. I don't remember Mom at all, and Dad always seemed bitter."

"Don't give up, Emma. Follow your instincts."

"Did you ever feel like quitting your job before you retired?"

She smiled. "At least once a month."

"Why didn't you?"

"Because the job, the calling, was more important than my feelings or my fears."

"Even when you made mistakes?"

"Especially when I made mistakes. If I had gotten a detail wrong in my investigation, it meant a criminal might go free. When I found myself in error, I worked harder to find the correct solution."

Rose picked up the tea tray with our empty cups and took it into the kitchen as I considered what she said. She was right, of course. I couldn't keep myself away from this investigation. And if the two deaths turned out to be a coincidence with no hint of murder, then I would celebrate being wrong.

But if I relied on those instincts Rose claimed I had, I wasn't wrong.

Nine

The next morning, I headed to the kitchen for my first cup of coffee. I poured the dark brew and lifted the cup, inhaling the rich aroma. I took my first sip and smiled. The day could start now.

Becky was pouring a lumpy mess into a Bundt cake pan.

"What's on the menu this morning?" I asked.

"I'm trying a new twist on an old favorite." She wiped the edge of the bowl with a spatula and scraped the last of the mess into the pan. "It's a breakfast casserole, but in a round pan instead of a nine by thirteen."

"Why?"

"If it turns out the way I planned, the servings will be in slices like cake."

I leaned on the prep counter as I sipped my coffee. "Fancy. You're getting more creative as time goes on."

Becky set the cake pan in an oven and set the timer. "I'd like to have six or seven recipes I can rotate from week to week. I'm trying a few out to see which ones the guests like best."

"Good idea."

She poured the last of the coffee into a mug and joined me at the counter. "What are your plans for today?"

"The usual. Breakfast for the guests, and then I need to tackle the housekeeping chores in the rooms. Why?"

"I thought we'd spend some time looking at the clues we've gathered."

"But we don't have anything new to add to the crime board, do we?"

A timer rang and Becky went to take a tray of burger buns out of the second oven and replace it with another pan of proofed buns.

"I think you'll want to work on it after breakfast anyway."

She was facing away from me, but from the tone of her voice I could tell something was up.

"What's going on?"

She transferred the buns to a cooling rack. "Just wait. I think you'll like it."

Becky's idea of making her casserole into a cake was brilliant. The savory bacon and cheese wrapped in the bread and egg casserole was flavored perfectly, and the presentation drew pleasant comments from the guests.

"Look at this," Betty Ann said. "It's cake for breakfast."

"What fun," Sally Marie said as she helped herself to a slice and added a serving of fresh berries to her plate. "Mama would die if she saw us having cake for breakfast, wouldn't she?"

As Betty Ann followed her sister to a table, she had a frown on her face. "But Sally Marie, Mama's already passed on. She couldn't die again, could she?"

Sally Marie took her seat with a long-suffering sigh. "It's only an expression. I know Mama's in heaven and has been for years."

Betty Ann set her plate on the table, but before she sat down, she cast a worried glance upward. "You don't suppose she's watching us right now, do you? I wouldn't want her to be upset about the cake."

The Thomas family came downstairs. Toni pushed her way past Taylor to get to the buffet first, but Ted pulled her back.

"Why don't you wait back here with me?" He held her close in a one-armed hug. "Let your mom go first this morning."

"But I'm hungry," Toni said.

"So is your mom." The Alberts and Walkers had followed them into the dining room and Ted let them go ahead. "And so are these fine people."

"But Dad-"

One look from Ted silenced her whine.

Soon everyone was accounted for, including Rose who had come in after taking Thatcher for his walk. Ted asked Rick and Debbie about their trip to Devils Tower the day before and the Brooks sisters were chatting to Joy about their shopping finds. Becky joined me at the buffet.

"This is the best part," she said.

"Watching people enjoy the fruits of your labors?"

"Yup." She glanced at the front door. "Gran always said the fun of running the café was watching people enjoy her food. I think I know what she means."

Her gaze went to the front door again.

"Are you waiting for someone?"

She grinned at me as the door opened. "And here

he is."

Cal pushed the door open, hauling one end of a large white board in a wooden frame on wheels. Becky ran to hold the door open. Another deputy was at the other end of the monstrosity.

"What is this?" I asked as I joined them at the bottom of the stairway.

"The department got some new equipment, and this was on its way out." Cal chewed on his toothpick. "I thought you could use it."

Becky grinned. "When he asked me about it, I told him you'd love it. No more poster board."

Rose had walked up to us. "I concurred with Becky."

"You knew about this, too?"

"Cal asked me about it a week ago, but it was his idea."

I glanced at Cal. His red cheeks and averted gaze were the only clues I had that he was worried about my reaction.

"I love it. But where are we going to put it?"

"In your suite." Becky bounced on her toes. "I know the perfect spot. Take it upstairs, guys."

My suite? Cal had already started up the steps with his end of the white board. My nice, clean, organized suite?

I followed Becky up the stairs. "Are you sure about this?"

"Perfectly." She let me catch up with her. "It can't be where anyone else can read it, and it should be where you can have access to it every time an idea strikes you. Your suite is the only place." She held out her hand. "Give me your key."

Helpless, I handed it to her. She slipped by Cal and

the other deputy and unlocked my door for them. I heard Tim's irritated meow, then they were in my living room. By the time I reached the door, Becky had already shown them the spot where she wanted it. Tim had disappeared into the bedroom.

Becky turned to me. "Isn't it perfect? Oh! I almost forgot." She reached into the pocket of her apron and pulled out a box of dry erase markers. "You'll need these. I got as many colors as I could. And I've got to go. Gran is waiting for her delivery."

The deputy followed Becky out, but Cal stayed behind, watching me. I made myself smile.

"Thank you, Cal. This was very thoughtful."

"You don't like it." He stalked into my kitchen and threw his toothpick in the trash. "I told Becky we should ask you first."

"No. I mean, yes. I like it."

"But?"

"But?"

"I heard a 'but' in there."

I considered the new addition. Becky had been right. It fit perfectly on the wall opposite the kitchenette, between the door and the French doors leading to the deck. It was far better than markers and a piece of poster board.

I shook my head. "No buts. I was just surprised. It's a wonderful gift."

"I wanted...well...I thought..." He took off his hat and gave me a softer look than I was used to. "You're a good detective. You helped a lot on the case last month, and when I saw this was for sale..." He jammed his hat back on his head. "A detective needs the right tools." He dug in his pocket and handed me some round metal objects. "It's magnetic, too."

I put one of the magnets on the white surface. The right tools. My throat grew tight.

"Thank you, Cal."

I turned toward him as he stepped close to put a second magnet on the board and nearly crashed into his chest. He steadied me the same as he had on the sidewalk the other day, but this time he didn't let me go. I risked a glance up at his face. His gaze went from my eyes to my lips. Time stopped as I took in a breath.

Then his eyes opened wide, and he released his hold. The moment was gone.

"Sorry. I didn't mean for that to happen."

I willed the trembling in my knees to stop. Cal was back to being Cal.

"It's okay."

"Okay?"

"Yeah." I looked back at the white board, trying to understand the swirling feelings. "Thanks for the white board." I took a deep breath and whooshed it out. "It's great. Professional."

He gave me a quick nod and let himself out. I closed the door behind him and leaned against it. Part of me wanted to swing the door open and chase him down to finish what he had started. Instead, I gave myself a mental shake. I could have been reading him all wrong.

But I hadn't panicked at the thought he might kiss me. I smiled to myself. That was progress. Maybe there was hope for me after my disastrous relationship with Bruce a couple years ago.

I turned back to the white board and placed the rest of the magnets on it. Small and round. Unobtrusive. Opening the package of markers Becky had left, I arranged them in the little trough below the white board. Ten colors. Perfect.

Tim came back into the living room with a questioning meow, winding between my ankles.

"Hey, buddy. Are you happier now that everyone else is gone?"

He sniffed the wooden stand with a delicate touch of his nose.

"Get used to it, Tim. I think it's going to stay."

He gave it a slap with his paw, then skittered away. When I saw him again, he was on his perch on the back of the sectional, his tail whipping from side to side.

I retrieved the poster board from under the ottoman. The information was sparse, but I set to work transferring it to the new white board.

When I had written Caro's name, I added the cause of death. "Poisoning by nicotine," I said as I wrote the words.

I stopped and replaced the cap on the marker, staring at what I had written. Somehow, I needed to find the connection between Caro and Mike. It was no coincidence the cause of death was the same for both of them.

I had just finished transferring the last of the information from our old crime board to the new one when Becky rapped on my door with the staccato pattern she always used. I opened the door.

"Come on in."

"You've started already!"

"I only put up the things we had already written on

the old board." I snapped the cap on the purple marker. "What do you think?"

She tipped her head to one side. "To make it really professional, we should use pictures of the victims and suspects."

"I'll let you work on that if you think we need them. I don't want to waste any time. If these were both murders, we need to find the culprit before he strikes again." I stepped back and took a good look at what I had written. "There isn't much to go on, is there?"

"The two deaths have one thing in common. The nicotine." Becky picked up a marker and underlined the word I had written below both victim's names. "But that's the only thing. Their lives don't intersect anywhere else."

"Yes, they do." I chose a blank spot in the middle of the board and started a list. "They were both in Paragon when they died."

"That isn't much to go on."

"No. But if we think, we can come up with more things. Anything."

"They both had businesses on Main Street."

I added it to the list. "And they were both seasonal residents, not year around."

Becky was silent, a frown on her face.

"What are you thinking about?"

"I'm wondering if they knew each other at all. Was Caro ever in Pete's Sammiches? Or was Mike ever at the art gallery?"

I started another list. "Perfect. Questions give us something to look for. We'll have to ask Pete if his brother ever met Caro."

"I can't think of anything else connecting them."

Becky said. She leaned against the back of the sectional. "We'd have a bigger list if we wrote down their differences."

"You're right. From what people have said, everyone liked Mike, but no one got along with Caro." I crossed my arms, thinking back over the past few days. "Except for Moose Morehead."

"Who?"

"The guy with the ponytail. Biker type. He was at the ice cream social."

"Oh, yeah. He was a friend of Caro's?"

"I'm not sure I'd call him a friend, but he might have been a business associate." I told her about finding the drugs in the bottom of the box Cal caught him removing from the gallery.

"Interesting."

"But even if Moose had killed Caro, why would he have killed Mike?"

"Maybe Mike saw something?"

"And Moose was afraid he would tell his brother?" I nodded and recorded that idea in a corner of the white board. It was a good thing we had room to work with. "That would give Moose a motive for both murders."

"That sounds too easy."

"Why can't the solution be simple? Not all murders are complex plots, are they?"

There was a tentative knock at my door. I looked at Becky. She shrugged. I opened the door.

Taylor was standing outside, twisting her fingers together. "Hi."

"Hi." I closed the door a little as she stood on her toes to see past me. "What's up?"

"I saw the deputy bringing in that big white board

and I was wondering what you were doing."

"Weren't you going sight-seeing with your family today?"

She leaned to one side, and I moved to block her view into my room.

"Not until lunch. Toni wanted her screen time, so Mom and Dad said we could hang around until then."

I glanced at Becky and got a shrug in response. "We're just talking." I smiled at Taylor, hoping she'd take the hint we were busy.

"I know what you're doing." Her voice dropped to a whisper. "You're solving the two murders, aren't you?"

"What makes you think there have been any murders?"

She ticked the items off on her fingers. "A crime board. You two holed up in the kitchen talking. And I know I heard you mention poison." She moved a step closer. "I can help. I grew up reading Nancy Drew, and I'm halfway through Agatha Christie's books." She narrowed her brown eyes. "You have to admit, that's a lot of detective stories."

I recognized the impatient longing and suppressed enthusiasm in her expression. I knew the feeling well.

"As long as your mom knows where you are. And you have to keep any details about the case to yourself."

At her eager nod I edged the door open slightly and she bounced into the room.

"I know I can help. What clues do we have so far?"

"Not many." Becky moved over so Taylor could lean on the back of the sectional next to her. "We've been trying to figure out if there's any connection between the two victims."

Taylor stared at the crime board, her head tilted to one side. "They don't have much in common, do they?"

"Not that we found," I said.

"And they were both poisoned?" Taylor leaned closer to the board. "What's this about a picture?"

"We found a picture next to the body in the first murder."

"But not in the second one?"

Becky and I exchanged glances. Taylor was right. I circled the info on the white board with my marker.

"If Caro was poisoned by the nicotine Cal found on the picture frame, then Mike's death might not be connected at all," I said.

"Except there was nicotine in his system," Becky said. "If he didn't have a picture, then how was he exposed to it?"

"But he did have one." I started writing the information under Mike's name as I talked. "Anna Grace said she gave one to him after he helped her in Living Wild on Sunday afternoon." I stood back and capped my pen. "But she said she wrapped it up for him before he went home."

"Then we're back to square one," Becky said. "Since it was wrapped up, he wouldn't have touched the frame."

"He would if he was anything like Toni," Taylor said.

"What do you mean?" I asked.

"Toni never leaves anything in its package. She has to take it out and play with it, even if it's a gift for someone else."

I turned back to the board again and underlined

what I had written. "Mike could have unwrapped the picture as soon as he got home, before he went to the ice cream social."

Becky checked her watch. "It's almost lunch time. It looks like the next thing to do is ask Pete if we can look at Mike's things. If we find the picture and it's unwrapped, then we have our murder weapon."

"Potential murder weapon," I said. "It looks like we're done here for now. I'll call Cal and see if he can make arrangements for us to stop by Pete's."

"Taylor?" Terri's voice drifted through the door as she knocked. "We're leaving now."

"Thanks for your help," I said as Taylor cast a longing glance at the white board.

"You'll let me know what you find out?"

"When we get more clues, we'll make sure you know about them." I opened the door. "As long as it's okay with your parents."

"She wasn't a bother?" Terri asked. "She insisted on spending time with you this morning."

"Not at all. She-" I stopped. How much should I tell Terri about our investigation?

Becky saved the day. "She's a whiz at puzzles and helped us figure out some sticky clues. It was fun, wasn't it, Taylor?"

"It sure was." Taylor grabbed her mom's arm and pulled her toward the stairway. "Come on, Mom. I'm hungry. Where are we going to go for lunch?"

"She's good," Becky said as they went to meet Ted and Toni downstairs.

"At solving mysteries or distracting her mother?"

"Both. See you this afternoon." She followed Taylor and Terri.

I closed the door behind her and went back to the

crime board. Tim came out of the bedroom and wound himself between my ankles until I picked him up.

"The clues might be making some sense," I said to him as I scratched his ears. "We'll know more after we visit Pete."

Tim batted at my chin until I put him down. It was time to call Cal.

Ten

Before I made a sandwich for my lunch, I gave Cal a call.

"Emma. I'm in a hurry. Is this important?" In spite of the near kiss earlier, his voice sounded like he was back to business.

I opened the French doors and walked out into the sunshine on the deck. "Becky and I have an idea we want to follow up on, but we need to look at Mike's stuff before we go any further with it."

"What is it?"

"It's about the picture Anna Grace gave Mike on Sunday afternoon. I think it's the same kind of picture we found with Caro's body. If Mike had one, that could have been the source of the nicotine."

I heard the sound of breaking dishes somewhere below me.

"Hold on, Cal."

Leaning over the edge of my balcony, I saw Charles and Violet on the deck outside their suite. It was to my right, separated from my aunt's deck by a screen of climbing roses that were beginning to leaf out. Charles was leaning over to pick up a plate Violet had dropped from shaking hands. Proud women hated for anyone to see their weaknesses, and I hoped she didn't know I had witnessed the accident. I went back into my suite and closed the door.

"Okay, I'm back."

"You were saying something about the source of the nicotine?"

"We want to see if Mike had one of those pictures. Could you contact Pete and see if it's all right for us to come over and look?"

"Sure. I'll call him this afternoon."

"Thanks."

The sound of tires spinning on gravel came through the phone. "Right now, I'm on my way to a call."

"Okay. Let me know when you're done."

"Better yet, I might need your help on this one. Can you meet me behind the art gallery?"

"Sure. Right now?"

"As soon as you can get there. I'll buy pizza for lunch."

I stared at my phone screen. Yes, he had hung up on me. Flashing lights down on the main road caught my eye. Cal's SUV. What was going on? I headed down to Paragon.

Main Street was packed with tourists even though the holiday weekend was over. The front door of the art gallery was still secured with crime scene tape, so I jogged around to the back and made my way around the brown and white deputy sheriff's vehicle. Cal stood right inside the back door of Old Time Photos, the shop next to the art gallery.

I stepped into the room next to him, but I couldn't go any farther. Broken cardboard boxes littered the floor, surrounded by piles of the pictures we had found on the day of Caro's death, the plastic packing sheets still intact. Cal's flashlight played over the mess, highlighting a layer of fine brownish dust covering everything. Footprints in the dust led to the door where we were standing.

"Wow. What happened?"

Cal's face was grim. "I got a call from one of my nephews. He noticed the back door standing open. Someone used a pair of bolt cutters to break in." He gestured in front of him. "This is what I found."

"What is this powder?" I reached down to swipe a finger through the film at my feet, but Cal stopped me.

"It looks like fentanyl." He pointed to a broken plastic packet like the ones we had found at the bottom of Moose's box on Saturday. "Somehow one of the bags got torn open."

"But I thought Moose had gotten that box from the art gallery."

"He did. Tyrone Jackson is usually in Paragon by now, but he hasn't opened his photo shop yet this year. It looks like Caro had been using his back room to store her stash. That would explain why CSU didn't find anything in the gallery."

I nodded. "The boxes in here are the same as the ones we found in the art gallery." I pointed to the flat wrapped packages that had been dumped out of the boxes. "But why would she keep them here instead of the art gallery?"

"These two stores are in the same building. At one time it was the school. Two rooms, one down and one up. Fifty or sixty years ago the school was closed, and the building was renovated into the two store fronts."

"I didn't see a connecting door or anything between them."

"Caro must have found some way to use this space."

I perused the room. "There is a stairway over there." I pointed to the corner on the right. "Where does it lead?"

Cal looked over my shoulder. "Upstairs to an apartment. That's where Tyrone lives when he's here for the season. The door under the stairs leads to the basement."

I looked around the room again. "Whoever broke in must have been in a hurry."

Cal looked at me, his eyes narrowed. "Why?"

"This stuff is expensive. If they thought they had the time, they would have swept it up. There must be hundreds of dollars of dust in this room."

"Thousands. And that makes me wonder how much was in here in the first place. They opened a dozen boxes or more."

"Who do you think broke in here?"

Cal's voice was a growl. "Moose Morehead is at the top of my list." He let the flashlight play over the debris again. "Do you see anything else?"

"It looks like only one person. Whoever did this was working alone."

"What makes you say that?"

"Look at the footprints. They're jumbled and confused like the person walked back and forth, but they're all the same. The size, the tread pattern."

Cal concentrated the light on the floor. "You're right." He turned toward me and the light shone in my face. "Two set of eyes are better than one. That's why I asked you to come over. What else do you see?"

I took the flashlight from him, pointed it into the corners of the room and back toward the center.

"Nothing else that stands out."

"Oh, man." Despair punctuated the exclamation from behind us.

We turned around to see Moose looking in the door. He took one look at Cal and turned to run. The chase didn't last long. Moose's bulk was against him, and he crashed to the ground under Cal's tackle within three strides. Cal cuffed him then pulled him to his feet.

"Well, hello Moose." Cal said. He picked Moose's ball cap off the gravel. "What brings you here today? Were you going to finish what you started?"

Moose shook his head. "No, man. You've got it all wrong."

"I do, huh? Why don't you set me straight, then?"

"I was walking by and wondered what was going on." He peered into the doorway again. "Did someone break into the art gallery, too? What did they take?"

Cal fished a toothpick out of his shirt pocket with his free hand. "I think you know what they were after. The same thing you were."

Moose's face turned red. "I don't know what you're talking about. I was just walking by."

"In the alley." The toothpick clenched between Cal's teeth accentuated the sarcasm. "Behind the art gallery. Come on. You know something about this, don't you?"

"No. I swear. Nothing."

"You didn't come by to recover the rest of the drugs yourself?"

Moose's voice grew sullen. "I don't know nothing about any drugs."

"I think we need to go to the office and talk about this."

Cal pulled Moose in the direction of the SUV.

"Wait." Moose tugged his elbow out of Cal's grasp.

"You're going to talk?"

"Maybe we can make a deal. I could tell you who did this." Moose gestured toward the photo shop door. "It wasn't me."

"Yeah? Then who was it?"

Moose looked from one end of the alley to the other. "I know Caro was involved in smuggling fentanyl. Find her partner and you've got your guy."

"Who is her partner?"

"I don't know. I only know Caro wasn't a dealer, so someone else must be."

Moose's gaze shifted toward the end of the alley again. He was nervous. I didn't see anything or anyone else around. Who was he afraid of?

"You know what I think?" The toothpick didn't move. "I think you know more than you're saying."

"I've told you everything I know." Moose's voice grew louder. "I don't have any idea who Caro's partner was. You can question me all you want, but you won't find out anything."

"Get in the car, Moose. You know the drill."

After another glance down the alley, Moose got into the back of the SUV without protest. Cal closed the door and walked back to me.

"What do think?"

"About Moose? He wasn't the one who broke in."

The toothpick bobbed. "Why not?"

"Did you see the size of his feet? He has to wear a size thirteen, at least. Those footprints are more like a size eight. Much smaller."

"A younger person."

"Or a woman. Or a smaller man."

The toothpick bobbed as Cal chewed on it. I waited.

"Any ideas who might be Caro's partner?"

I shook my head. "It could be anybody, couldn't it?"

Cal sighed. "Everyone is a suspect."

"But whoever it is could also be our murderer."

His eyes narrowed. "You still think Caro's death is a murder?"

"After this, I'm convinced of it. Something went wrong between Caro and her partner, and she paid the price."

"And where do you get this theory?"

I bit my lower lip. I couldn't tell him I had read that same plot in the mystery I had finished reading the other night.

"It makes sense, doesn't it?"

"There is only one problem." The toothpick didn't move. "I've never heard of a drug dealer using poison to take care of his personnel problems. Guns, yes. Vehicular assault, yes. Poison? Never."

It wasn't until after Cal drove away with Moose in the back seat that I remembered the deputy had promised pizza for lunch.

"Thanks, Cal."

A sound from the house on the other side of the

alley made me look up in time to see the curtain in the second-floor window fall back into place. Someone had been watching me. Had that person been watching the entire time? They could have beene a witness to the break in.

I reached for my phone, then stopped myself. What if that person was Caro's partner? Trying to look casual, as if I hadn't seen that curtain move, I walked to the end of the alley and turned onto Willow Street. Once I was past the corner of Gran's house and out of sight of that window, I hit the button to call Cal.

"Hey, Emma. Did I forget something?"

Yeah. Lunch.

"No. I only thought I'd let you know someone had been watching us from the house across the alley from the gallery. Do you know who lives there?"

"That's a vacation rental. Do you think they saw something?"

"I thought they might be a witness to the break-in, or else..." I hesitated. It was only my speculation Moose had been afraid of being seen with Cal.

"Or else what?" Cal sounded impatient.

"Nothing. I'll talk to you later."

"Okay. Gotta go."

He hung up and I stared at the screen. Someone got cranky when he missed his lunch.

Just like me. I threaded through the traffic on Main Street and headed up to the Sweetbrier. I could use some lunch, too.

After a quick tuna salad sandwich, I started making my rounds of the guest rooms. Keeping my hands busy would help me think.

While I was gathering the supplies I needed from

the upstairs linen closet, I heard Violet and Charles leaving. I'd hurry and take care of their room first. There was no telling how long they would be gone.

As I made the bed and switched clean towels for the used ones, I couldn't help noticing the number of bottles on the bathroom vanity. Some were pills and some were liquids. A glance at some of the labels showed many of them were supplements or vitamins, rather than medications. A couple were blank. I would have labeled everything so I wouldn't get them mixed up.

Then I went upstairs to the Dublin Bay where Betty Ann and Sally Marie were staying. Their room was easy to take care of. The sisters had emptied their suitcases into the closet and dresser drawers. Their bed was already made, and the used towels hung neatly on the bars in the bathroom. I smiled as I switched the towels for clean ones, imagining their mother drilling good housekeeping habits into her daughters. Habits that had lasted the rest of their lives.

The two connecting rooms the Thomas family occupied were also neat, although I could tell that Ted and Terri were occupying the Snow Goose while Taylor and Toni shared the Albertine. The bed in the first room had been made with military precision and the bathroom was spotless, while the Albertine held evidence of the girls' possessions everywhere.

As I changed the towels and wiped down the sink and vanity surfaces, I mused about how much I knew about our guests from spending a few minutes in their rooms. If one of them was a criminal, would I be able to tell from the clues they left behind?

Stopping at the linen closet at the top of the stairs

to grab more clean towels, I went on to the Westerland, Joy and Dave Albert's room.

I made the bed, exchanged the towels for clean ones, then did a quick dusting. When I reached the dresser with my feather duster, I paused and looked at the picture on display. It was one from Living Wild. A print of a fern, the same type we found next to Caro's body. Was this one covered with nicotine residue, too? I didn't touch it but looked closely at the frame. The surface was shiny, almost oily. Or was that only my imagination? Leaving the picture where it was, I went on to the Rambling Rector, Rick and Debbie Walker's room. They also had one of the pictures displayed on the nightstand. Next to it was one of those spray bottles used for allergies that would deliver a measured dose into the patient's nostrils.

I looked closer at the warning label. It wasn't for allergies. It was a product to help someone quit smoking. The warning was to use it only as directed to avoid nicotine poisoning.

Nicotine poisoning? My fingers grew cold at the implication. Could this be the source of the nicotine that killed Caro and Mike? I took a picture of the bottle, hoping neither Debbie nor Rick could be murderers, in spite of this evidence.

I put the phone back in my pocket, considering what I knew of the couple. Debbie was passionate about her art and Rick was the type who would indulge his wife's passions no matter where they led her. But would her passionate nature lead her to murder? And what could be their motive? I hated to entertain the thought, but there was possible evidence right in front of me. It was something else to discuss with Cal.

Closing the door of the Rambling Rector behind me, I made sure it was locked, then put my cleaning supplies in the closet and gathered up the soiled towels to take to the laundry room. It was already three o'clock and time to get ready for afternoon tea.

Charles and Violet had returned while I was working and were in the dining room when I came downstairs. Violet was sipping from a cup of tea while she watched Charles work on a jigsaw puzzle from the inn's library. I greeted them on my way to the laundry room and received a wave in return.

I started the washing machine, then went into the kitchen where Becky was pulling a tray of scones out of the oven.

"Hey, girl," she said. "What's wrong?"

"What makes you think something is wrong?"

"I know you." She pointed her spatula at me. "You've got that look that says you're trying to figure out something."

I leaned against the counter, my arms crossed. "Those pictures from Living Wild. I thought finding one next to Caro's body was a clue that would lead somewhere, but they're all over the place."

Becky slipped a warm scone onto a napkin and handed it to me. "Where else did you find them?"

"There's the one Anna Grace gave to Mike, and then I found a couple more as I was cleaning the guest rooms."

"Could all of them be poisoned?"

"I hope not." I broke off a corner of the scone and popped it in my mouth. Mmm. Cream cheese and vanilla. "But we'll have to ask Cal to check them out."

The sound of a metal spoon on a China cup came from the other side of the buffet shutter, telling me

Charles was making another cup of tea. I moved closer to Becky and lowered my voice. "What bothers me, though, is that I found a nicotine nasal spray bottle in Rick and Debbie's room."

"Like the kind you use to stop smoking?"

I nodded. "I hope it isn't the source of the poison. I like that couple."

"But what would their connection be with either of the victims?"

"That's just it. I have no idea, but I'll keep looking."

With the nasal spray still on my mind, I went out to set up the dining room for tea. Violet was sitting alone at her table, sorting through the puzzle pieces.

I started a pot of coffee, then took a carafe of hot water over to Violet.

"Would you like some more water for your tea?"

"Yes, thank you." She pushed her nearly empty cup toward me.

"You're making good progress on your puzzle."

Violet's hand shook as she attempted to pick up one of the pieces. She succeeded on her third try and pressed it into place, then she gave me a smile. "Charles and I always have a puzzle set up at home. It's one of the few things we can do together."

"But he left you to finish this one on your own."

I grinned, turning my comment into a friendly tease, but Violet stiffened, then gestured vaguely toward their suite.

"He had something to take care of." Her eyes were hard as she looked at me, but her smile remained. "He'll be back soon."

"Becky made cream scones today. They are so light and delicious, you'll love them. I'll bring you some when they're ready."

Her expression softened. "Thank you."

I left her to her puzzle and continued setting up the buffet with plates, napkins, and silverware. I was refilling the various sweeteners when Rose and Thatcher came out of her suite.

"You're just in time for tea," I said as I leaned down to scratch Thatcher's ears. He smiled at me, his tongue lolling sideways.

"I could smell the scones baking from my office." Rose put on her hat and patted her leg for Thatcher to follow her. "We'll be back soon."

But the corgi paused at the bottom of the stairway and gruffed. When Rose patted her leg again, he looked at her and whined.

"What's wrong?" I joined him at the bottom of the stairs. "You go take Rose on her walk and don't worry about the guest rooms."

He took one more look toward the second floor, then followed Rose out the door. What had Thatcher been worried about upstairs? I had my foot on the bottom step when Violet called to me.

"Emma, I'm sorry to bother you, but I could use some assistance."

I glanced up the stairs one more time, but I hadn't heard anything. Thatcher must have been imagining things this time. I hurried into the dining room.

"What can I help you with?"

"I'm so clumsy sometimes. I was reaching across the puzzle and knocked all those pieces on the floor. Could you pick them up for me?"

"Sure. No problem." On the other side of Violet's wheelchair more than a dozen puzzle pieces were scattered on the floor and I knelt to pick them up.

"It's frustrating when that happens, isn't it?"

But Violet wasn't upset by the incident. "It happens more often than you would think." She pointed with a shaking hand. "I think one went under the table."

I had placed all the stray pieces back on the table when the Thomas family returned. Toni ran over to me.

"Emma, look!" She held up a tiny glass vial with a few glowing yellow grains in the bottom. "It's real gold!"

"Wow! Where did you find that?"

Toni grinned. "We went to a gold mine, and they taught us how to pan for gold. We all found some!"

"That's great. It sounds like a lot of fun." I glanced at Taylor, who was standing behind her sister with her own vial. "Did you enjoy it as much as Toni?"

She looked like she was trying hard not show her own excitement. "It was okay."

Terri put one arm around Taylor's shoulder. "You should have heard her when she found the gold in her pan. She squealed louder than Toni."

"I'm going to keep mine forever," Toni said.

"Let's go upstairs and get cleaned up before we have our tea. Your dad wants to go to the Crazy Horse site this evening."

As Terri and Toni followed Ted upstairs, Taylor hung back. "Have I missed anything? Have you found any more clues?"

Violet was watching us, her eyes bright and interested. "Clues?"

Taylor grimaced when she realized we had an audience.

"It's a game we're playing," I told Violet. "One of

those mystery games, like Clue." I tried to reassure Taylor with a smile. "Come find me after you get back from your visit to Crazy Horse and we'll pick it up again."

Taylor followed her family upstairs and I went into the kitchen. Becky was placing the scones on the serving tray. She had drizzled frosting on the tops since I taste-tested one earlier. At four o'clock I opened the shutter over the buffet and we set the scones on the counter along with a pitcher of iced tea. The Brooks sisters had returned while I was in the kitchen, along with Dave and Joy. Rick and Debbie had come in and joined the others at the buffet.

I couldn't hear my phone ring over their chatter, but I felt the vibration in my back pocket and pulled it out. Cal. I went into the utility room where I would have some privacy.

"Hey, Cal."

"Hey. Your tip on the possible witness didn't pan out. The guy said he wasn't home when the break-in happened. He didn't see anything."

"Sorry. I thought they might have."

"I have to follow every lead, and it might have been a good one."

"Did you call Pete?"

"Yup. He's expecting us at ten o'clock tomorrow morning. Although I'm sure it's a waste of time. Mike died from natural causes."

"But he had nicotine in his system, the same as Caro. That can't be a coincidence."

"I'm chasing down leads on the drug angle, and that's where the trail is leading. CSU found a lot of evidence at the photo shop."

"Anything you can share with me?"

"Not yet. Not this close to solving the case. Do you want me to pick you up in the morning, or should we meet me at Pete's?"

"I'll meet you. The walk will do me good."

"Sure thing. See you there."

I put my phone away but didn't go back out to the dining room yet. It sounded like Cal had discounted the nicotine poisoning in his investigation. Was he right? He might be. He certainly had more experience than me.

But I couldn't ignore the nagging pull of the evidence. The causes of death. The exposure to nicotine. It wasn't making any sense. Where was the connection to the drugs we found at the photo shop?

I rubbed my temples to clear my head. It all depended on what we found at Mike's place in the morning.

Eleven

The next morning, I met Cal at Pete's Sammiches at ten o'clock on the dot. His SUV was already parked in the alley and he was leaning on the front fender.

"Enjoying the weather?" I asked him as I got closer.

He tossed his toothpick into the nearby trash bin and grabbed his duffel bag from the hood of the vehicle. "If it wasn't for these deaths we're investigating, I would be."

I took in the cloudless blue sky above us. "If this perfect day hasn't distracted you from your investigation, you must think you're getting close to solving it."

"Yup. And it has nothing to do with picture frames and nicotine. CSU found fingerprints at the photo shop, and we have a suspect."

"Who?"

"Not going there. With drugs involved this whole thing is getting too dangerous. It's time for you to step back and let the department finish up."

"But we're still going to see if Mike's picture was poisoned with nicotine, right?"

Cal adjusted his hat and walked with me up the outside stairway to Pete's back door. "Since I know you won't let this line of investigation go until we find out for sure, yes. But this is the end. The nicotine is a distraction. A fluke."

"You mean a coincidence? I thought you didn't believe in coincidences."

"I don't. And I don't think we're going to find any trace of nicotine on anything Mike owns."

He knocked on the door and Pete answered. The haunted look was gone and he was dressed in a polo shirt and khakis.

"Hey. Come on in."

"How are things going?" Cal said.

"Not too bad, considering." Pete led us past the kitchen and into his living room. The liquor bottles were gone. "Anna Grace has helped a lot. She's been through something similar with the death of her husband and listened while I talked about Mike. I still miss him like crazy, though."

"Have you made plans for the funeral?" I asked.

"Yeah. I'll take him home to bury him with our parents and have a memorial service."

Cal ticked his hat brim up. "When are you planning to do this?"

"I'd like to go this week, or as soon as I can make the arrangements."

"You need to stick around until we finish up the investigation."

"Investigation?"

"I want to be certain Mike died from natural causes before we release him to you. You understand."

Pete sat down. "Sure. Sure. Whatever you need."

"Do you mind if we look at his things?" Cal asked.

Pete waved toward a short hallway toward the front of the building. "His room is on the left. I haven't even gone in there since it happened." He grabbed a tissue out of a box on the couch and blew his nose. "Sorry. I guess I'm still emotional about it."

"Don't worry about it," I said. "Give yourself some time."

Cal turned on the light as we entered the room, leaving Pete in the living room. The single bed was neatly made, and a pair of shoes was tucked under the edge. In the middle of the bed was a picture like the one Caro had been holding when she died.

"That's it," I said. "The picture Anna Grace gave him as a thank you for helping her in the store on Sunday afternoon."

I reached to pick it up, but Cal stopped me.

"We need to do this properly if we're going to do it," he said. He removed two pairs of gloves from his duffel bag and we both put them on. He also removed a flat plastic box.

"What's that?"

"A test kit. We'll be able to tell if there's nicotine present without having to bother the lab."

I stood back while Cal performed the simple test.

"Well?" He was taking too long as he looked at the results.

"It's positive. There is definitely nicotine on this picture frame." He slid the picture into a plastic evidence bag from his duffel. "I'll send this to the lab to get a more accurate result."

"Did you find something?" Pete asked from the doorway.

I jumped. I thought he was still waiting in the

living room.

Cal stripped off his gloves. "We'll need to take this picture into the lab. Just a formality. We'll return it to you when the investigation is done."

"Don't bother. If that's what killed my brother, I don't want to see it again."

Cal caught my eye and tilted his head toward the door. It was time to go.

"Thank you for your help," I said as I sidled past Pete.

"You're welcome." Pete ran his hand through his hair as he watched us leave. "Do you need anything else from me?"

"Not at this time." Cal pulled another toothpick from his shirt pocket. "I'll keep you updated on the investigation so you can make your plans."

"I appreciate it."

Pete closed the apartment door behind us. Cal didn't say anything but held the passenger door of his SUV open for me. I got in and waited until he was settled in the driver's seat and had started the engine before I asked the question thrumming through my brain.

"Now that we know where Mike came into contact with the nicotine that killed him, what's next?"

Cal put the vehicle in gear and started down the alley. "An early lunch. I owe you pizza. We can discuss the case while we eat."

He drove to the convenience store at the edge of town and parked in front of the store. "We'll grab the pizza and a couple drinks and take it up into the Hills. I know a great spot a couple miles up the road."

"It's a beautiful day for a picnic."

"It is. And the place is secluded." He opened the door. "No one will hear as we discuss the case."

His last comment was like a cold bucket of water on the perfect romantic lunch my imagination had been building. I sighed and opened my own door to follow him into the store. With Cal, it was all business where his job was concerned.

After getting a pepperoni pizza and a couple waters, we got back in the SUV and headed into the Hills up Mackenzie's Draw Road. The gravel road was steep for the first few hundred yards, then turned and leveled off to follow the crest of a ridge. A few yards before the road took a steep drop on the other side, Cal pulled off on a wide spot. He parked so the view through the windshield overlooked Paragon. Across the valley the Sweetbrier Inn glowed honey-brown in the trees.

"Wow. I've never seen Paragon from this high up."

"Let's sit on that log over there," Cal said, taking the pizza box from me. "You grab the drinks."

The log was gray and weathered, smooth from years of rain and wind. We sat down and each took a piece of pizza.

"Okay," I said before I took my first bite. "If both Mike's picture and Caro's had nicotine residue on the frame, that means someone had to put it there, right?"

Cal nodded, his mouth full.

"The question is who." I took a bite. The pizza was delicious.

"The first thing to look at is if those pictures came from the factory already tainted. Neither one had enough nicotine to kill a normal person."

"But enough to make someone sick. If the manufacturer was doing it, wouldn't other customers have reported it?"

"If they knew that was the cause." Cal took another bite.

"I have a couple other ideas of who could have done it, but I hate to think either party had anything to do with murder."

"Who?"

I glanced at him, suddenly reluctant to voice my suspicions. "Well, I found nicotine nasal spray in Rick and Debbie Walker's room when I was cleaning yesterday."

"A dose of that spray doesn't contain much nicotine. I don't think it would be strong enough even to make someone ill. But I'll check into it." He finished his slice, tossing a bit of the crust to a curious chipmunk who darted out to retrieve it. "You said you had a couple ideas."

"The other one is Anna Grace."

"The pictures came from her store," Cal said. "That would be too obvious."

"That's true. And she doesn't seem like the type, does she? But-" A sudden thought made me clamp my mouth closed. I didn't even want to think about the possibility that flashed through my mind.

"But what."

"It's nothing. Just a suspicion."

"That's why we're here, Emma. We have to examine every possibility so we can shut down this line of investigation for good."

"Okay. What if..." My stomach clenched at the thought. "What if Anna Grace and Pete worked together to...well...hurry Mike's death along. Pete said he had outlived the doctors' expectations."

"Why would they do that?"

I shuddered. "To start a new life together without Mike around. Maybe they thought he was a burden."

Cal didn't say anything. He stared across the valley.

"I know. It's terrible to think about it, isn't it? I mean, would someone actually do something like that outside of a murder mystery?"

"You'd be surprised what people will do out of selfishness or greed." He picked up a second piece of pizza. "I might check to see if Mike had a life insurance policy." He ate half the pizza in his hand, then took a drink. "But that doesn't explain Caro's death. What did she have to do with Anna Grace and Pete?"

He was right. Anna Grace and Pete couldn't have murdered Mike. I was so relieved at his words that I could have kissed him. Instead, I picked up my second slice and took a bite, but my relief was premature as Cal continued.

"Unless they poisoned several of those pictures to provide a decoy. Rose said the dosage for someone with a heart condition would be lower than for anyone else, and Mike's health wasn't a secret."

I put the last of my pizza back in the box and wiped my fingers on a napkin. My stomach felt like a rock had sunk to the bottom.

Cal ate the last of his slice then pointed to my half-eaten slice. "You're done?"

I nodded and finished my bottle of water. Everything was sour.

"Tell you what," he said as he closed the box and stood up. "You go to Living Wild and ask Anna Grace about those pictures. Gauge her reaction.

Meanwhile, I'll keep working on the drug angle." He glanced at me. "Don't worry. I'm sure your theory is wrong and you'll prove it when you talk to Anna Grace."

I put the cap on my empty bottle and got to my feet. "Thanks for the pizza."

"You're welcome." He looked out at the view once more. "We'll have to do it again sometime. Maybe when we aren't working on a case."

I couldn't enjoy the view, knowing I needed to question Anna Grace to put my suspicions to rest, but Cal's comment had opened a door to possibilities for the future.

"Sure. I'd like that."

Living Wild was busy when Cal dropped me off at the door. Vacationers crowded the spaces between the displays so thickly that the only way to navigate was to follow the flow around the store. As I went, I noticed a few new displays, but none of the pictures that had filled an entire shelf over the weekend. Had Anna Grace hidden the evidence?

The flow of customers finally eased enough that I could make my way to the cash wrap station on the other side of the room. Anna Grace's smile was contagious as she chatted with customers and rang up their purchases. She certainly didn't look like a guilt-ridden soul with murder on her conscience.

"Hi, Emma!" Her smile grew wider when she saw me. "Can I help you find anything?"

I willed myself to relax as I returned her smile. "I was looking for one of those pictures. You know, like the one you gave to Mike. I love the design and a couple would look great on my living room wall."

Her smile disappeared. "I'm sorry. I sold the last of those pictures yesterday. Someone came in and bought the rest of my stock. I'm glad I received more merchandise to fill in the space."

"That's too bad." Was she telling the truth? Her eyes didn't shift away from mine as we talked, even though another customer was approaching the cash register. "I'll let you get back to your other customers." I leaned closer and dropped my voice. "Pete told me how talking with you helped him over the past couple days."

Her cheeks grew pink. "He's a pretty special guy. I don't think I've ever met anyone like him. I thought my husband was perfect, but Pete is perfect in a different way."

I said goodbye as she turned to the next customer. It didn't seem like my suspicion was correct, and I left Main Street feeling better than I had since the thought of Anna Grace and Pete conspiring together entered my mind. But now I was back to zero.

Maybe Cal was right and Caro's murder was tied to the drugs we found at the gallery. But where did that leave Mike's murder?

If it was murder, my brain echoed.

The key had to be those pictures. It was too much of a coincidence that Caro and Mike both had high levels of nicotine in their blood and had both come into contact with one of those pictures.

But what did that have to do with Caro's drug smuggling, if that was what she had been doing?

And why did the clues keep leading me back to Anna Grace?

As I waited for traffic to clear before crossing the highway, I let my mind replay the scene in Living Wild. When I asked Anna Grace about the pictures, had she seemed edgy? I didn't get the feeling she was lying, but maybe she had been hiding something from me.

I crossed the street and started walking up Graves' Gulch Road to the inn.

Did she know who had purchased the rest of her stock of those pictures and why?

And what did Caro have to do with them?

When I arrived at the inn the dining room was empty and Becky was coming out of the kitchen.

"Hey girl."

"Hey."

"What's up?"

"Do you want to do some internet sleuthing with me?"

"Sure thing. I have bread dough rising, but it still has a couple hours to go." We went up the stairs. "Who are we investigating?"

"I think we need to take another look at Caro's life. I can't figure out where she fits in. Cal is convinced it has something to do with smuggling drugs from China."

Becky leaned on the door frame as I unlocked the door. "But you aren't, are you?"

I shook my head as the door swung open. "If that's the key, then why was Mike killed? And if I'm right about Anna Grace and Pete, then why was Caro killed?"

"What? Anna Grace and Pete?"

I filled her in on my theory. "But I doubt if that's what really happened."

"Or maybe you don't want it to be true."

"You're right about that." I picked up Tim for a quick cuddle as I reviewed the crime board. "Either one of those theories could solve the case, but both have problems. There has to be something we're missing."

"You mentioned internet sleuthing?"

I put Tim on the back of the couch and set my computer on the ottoman. Becky sat next to me.

"We've looked at Caro's website, but I thought we should look further into her life before she arrived in Paragon." I brought up Caro's website. "Where should we start?"

"Let's start at the beginning. Wasn't there a page with her bio? Where did she go to school again?"

I found the name of the school in Caro's biography, opened a new window and did a search.

"Here it is. Forestgreen Academy of Art." I clicked on the link.

"Hmm." Becky pointed at the menu bar. "Click on that page. Alumni."

I clicked on the link and a list of names appeared. "It looks like they have listed everyone who has ever attended the school."

"Scroll down and see if you can find Caro."

The list was alphabetical, and I clicked on Caro's name. A new page popped up. "It's a profile page."

Becky shifted closer to see the screen better. "There's her picture and a link to her website."

"And here's a link called 'awards and honors.' I wonder what they listed there."

The new page listed artist in residence programs she had led, starting with the most recent. As I scrolled down, classes she had taught at the school were highlighted. Then came a series of pictures from when she had been a student at Forestgreen.

I clicked on one of the photos to enlarge it. In the center of the picture was an unfinished painting. It looked like *Almost Spring*, the painting I had seen above the desk in the art gallery. A young Caro stood on the left side wearing a painter's smock. Part of another figure stood on the right-hand side of the painting.

"Is that other person blocked out?" Becky leaned forward. "It looks like the photo has been cropped. I can only see part of her."

"You're right. She's almost cropped out altogether. You know, if her head and shoulder didn't cover the edge of the painting, she would have been completely removed." I looked closer. "She looks familiar."

"You can only see part of her face."

"Still..."

The young woman was unusually tall and thin. Her head was tilted slightly, as if she was leaning into the painting. On her face was an expression of pride and joy.

"She looks like Violet."

"Violet Bishop?"

I tilted my head to match the one in the photo. "It's the eyes. It sure looks like a young version of Violet."

"What would she be doing in a picture of Caro with her painting?"

"I don't know. But if this is Violet in the picture, then she must have been a student at the same school as Caro. It looks like they might have even been friends."

"That's weird. She didn't say anything when Caro

died. She didn't react to the news at all. It could have been a stranger who had died."

"Maybe we're wrong and that isn't Violet in the picture."

I scrolled to the next picture. It was of a group of students on the steps of a large building.

"That's the Art Institute of Chicago. See the sign behind them?" Becky pointed. "There's Caro. And that same tall thin girl is next to her."

"Now that I can see her better, I'm not certain that's Violet."

Becky squinted. "It could be, I guess."

"I'm going to save these two photos to my computer and then we'll check the alumni list again."

A few clicks of my mouse and we were back to the list of alumni. I scrolled down the list.

"No Violet Bishop," Becky said.

"But she's married now. She would be listed under her maiden name, right?"

I went to the top and scrolled slowly, looking at every first name.

When we got to the end of the list, Becky said, "That's it then. Even if that person looks like Violet, it can't be her. It was a good idea, but a dead end." She stood up. "I have to get back to work. We're having oat and honey scones for tea."

I shut my laptop, trying to shut out my disappointment at the same time. "We'll work on this later. Meanwhile, I'll see if Rose will print these pictures for us."

It was too early in the afternoon to disturb Rose's writing, so I stopped at the registration desk and checked the inn's website. There were two more reservations for October. Rose had decided to close the season at the end of October instead of the beginning as she had previous years, and it looked like it was a worthwhile experiment. So far, we had reservations every weekend. I confirmed the new bookings then shared a post from Custer State Park on our social media sites.

A few minutes later the door to Rose's suite opened. I picked up my laptop and met her as she came out. She had Thatcher's leash in her hand and the corgi jumped on my knees to greet me.

"Emma! Have you been waiting for me?"

I told Thatcher to sit before rewarding him with an ear rub. "I have something to show you, but I can wait until you and Thatcher get back."

"I'll tell him to be quick. Go wait in my suite and I'll be back in a minute."

I took my computer in and set it on Rose's coffee table. By the time I had brought up the photos I had saved, she and Thatcher had returned. He jumped onto the couch next to me and angled his body against my leg. He pointed his black button nose toward the computer as if he was examining the photo on the laptop screen.

Rose sat on my other side and I turned the laptop toward her so she could see the picture of Caro with the painting better.

"This is from Caro's time at school."

Thatcher climbed over my lap to lay between us.

"That's an interesting painting." Rose angled her head. "But it looks unfinished."

"I think it's the one that's hanging on the wall in Caro's gallery. The name on the painting is *Almost Spring*. The composition is very similar to this, but it's complete. The finished work has a lot more green in it."

"It's quite abstract."

"But that isn't what I wanted to show you. Do you recognize the two women?"

"The one on the left is Caro, isn't it?" I nodded and Rose went on. "But the woman on the right is obscured. I can't positively identify her."

I clicked to bring up the second picture. "How about this one?"

"It looks like a class field trip to the Art Institute of Chicago, and there's Caro again."

"Does anyone else look familiar?"

Rose scooted forward and put on a pair of reading glasses. "Yes, I think you're right." She pointed to a short blond in the front row. "Isn't that Debbie Walker?"

"Becky and I had been so focused on Caro that we hadn't looked at the rest of the group." I leaned forward, too. "I think you're right. She still wears her hair in that same style."

"You sound surprised."

"I hadn't considered I'd recognize anyone else in the picture. I thought you might recognize this woman." I pointed to the tall thin woman standing next to Caro.

"She looks familiar. Something about her face."

"Does she remind you of Violet Bishop?"

"Yes. That's it." Rose removed her glasses and gave me a thoughtful look. "She has changed a lot, if it's her."

"The problem is that we looked through the alumni list from the art academy Caro attended, but there is no Violet on the list."

Rose tapped her glasses against her chin. "That's

interesting." She stared at the picture for another minute, then stood. "Would you like me to print those photos for you?"

"That would be great. I can put them on my new crime board."

She connected to her printer through the inn's wi-fi and we soon heard it working.

I followed Rose to her office, stopping at the doorway until she said, "Come in, Emma. I have no secrets from you."

Rose kept her office door closed and locked at all times. When I stepped in, I felt like Mary must have when she first found the Secret Garden. Bookshelves lined one wall and lateral file cabinets filled the space under the windows. Rose's desk was in the center of the room. She took the pictures from the printer tray and handed them to me.

"How is your new crime board working out?"

"It's perfect. But I don't know why Cal thought of giving it to me."

"I think he's interested in you."

I looked up from the photo I was examining. "You mean, like romantically?"

She smiled. "Are you surprised?"

"I don't know. Sometimes I think he's being friendly, and other times he's all business."

"It was the same way with Harry and I at first. The investigation always came first. But we managed to fall in love in spite of that."

Love? I went back to the living room and retrieved my laptop. Rose couldn't think Cal and I would ever have the kind of love she had shared with Uncle Harry.

But that almost-kiss moment? The idea was

intriguing.

Twelve

I went to sleep that night dreading the next morning, and my dreams didn't help. I woke up groggy with a distinct memory of chasing Anna Grace down Paragon's Main Street, dodging framed pictures thrown at me by the crowds on the sidewalks.

My morning shower did nothing to dispel the haunting terror of the nightmare. I lectured myself in the mirror.

"It was just a dream," I said as I rinsed my toothbrush.

"It wasn't real," I said as I brushed my hair.

I peered at my reflection. My simple hairdo, short, straight, and swept back from my face in layers, was looking shaggy.

I sighed as the dream came rushing back into my mind. That quick distraction hadn't been enough.

In the dining room I started the coffee maker with the smooth roast the guests enjoyed, then went into the kitchen to grab my cup of Rattlesnake blend. I inhaled the steam from my cup in a long, deep breath.

That was better.

"Rough night?" Becky was busy at the prep

counter with a pile of bananas.

"I had a bad dream. I can't shake the dreadful feeling it gave me."

She gave me a sympathetic look. "I hate when that happens." She peeled one of the bananas.

"What are you making?" I took a sip of my coffee.

"Banana Boats." She cut the banana in half and laid it on a rectangular plate.

"It looks like you're making a banana split."

"That's the idea." She pointed at the bowls of ingredients on the counter one by one. "The banana is the base, then a spoonful of vanilla Greek yogurt topped with granola. And then I'll sprinkle the whole thing with blueberries and strawberries. The last thing are these tiny chocolate chips."

"The guests are going to love those."

She grinned. "I think so, too. We're also having English sausage rolls and baked eggs."

"Perfect for a summer morning."

Becky peeled another banana. "Tell me about this dream. It wasn't about Cal, was it?"

"Anna Grace was in it. In my dream I knew she was the murderer, but she was running away and laughing at me." I picked up a blueberry. "No, not laughing. Cackling. Like a wicked witch."

"What brought it on?"

"I think I'm dreading having to talk to her again. I like her and I think we could be good friends, but I can't get rid of the suspicion she's involved in these deaths somehow."

"But yesterday you didn't think she was. You can't let a dream influence the investigation."

I took another drink of my coffee. "Did anyone ever tell you how wise you are? You are so right."

"Of course, I am." Becky grinned at me again. "Just put that dream out of your mind. When are you going to see Anna Grace?"

"I'll go down to her store after breakfast, before she opens for the day. We should be able to avoid interruptions then."

"Do you want some company? I was thinking about texting Ashley to see if she wanted to do lunch."

"That's a great idea. You don't think she'll be too busy today?"

She gave me her Becky look. A mixture of exasperation and humor.

"Girl, you've never been here during the tourist season. June is quiet compared to July and August. If we're going to do lunch in the summer, it's got to be now."

All the guests were early for breakfast and the banana boat bar was a hit. Becky had placed the split bananas on plates and the toppings in bowls so each guest could create their own.

Toni giggled as she put three spoonfuls of chocolate chips on top of her creation. Taylor rolled her eyes at her younger sister's antics, but I noticed she sprinkled the chocolate chips liberally, too. After she set her breakfast on the table, she came over to me.

"How is the investigation going?" she asked, her voice a whisper as she picked up a napkin from the end of the buffet. "Do you have any more leads?"

"The police have gotten involved, so we're staying out of it for now."

She gave me a sideways look. "Really? You're letting it go that easily?"

"Yes. The deputy is following a line of inquiry involving some pretty dangerous stuff."

"Okay, Emma. If you say so."

"What does that mean?"

"I've read enough mysteries to know there is always more than one trail to follow. You're letting the police handle the dangerous stuff, but you're still following your nose, aren't you?" She picked up a spoon and a fork. "I wish we were staying at the inn today so I could help you."

"There isn't much to do. I'm going to make a couple inquiries in town today, but I'm pretty sure I'll only find more dead ends."

"Are you going to be going through the clues tonight? Maybe we'll get home early enough that I can help."

I gave her a smile I hoped looked reassuring. "That would be great, but I don't want you to miss any of your family time. There are more important things than sifting through clues again."

Taylor glanced over at her family. Her dad was teasing Toni about something and all three of them were laughing. "We're having a good time." She wrapped her spoon and fork in the napkin. "At home, my mom and dad are always busy with work, and Toni and I have school and sports and stuff. But here, we're together all the time. And we're having fun."

"I'm glad you are. But you sound surprised."

"If you had told me last week that I'd enjoy spending the day with my little sister, I would have said you were nuts. But she's a pretty cool kid."

"You know something, Taylor? You are, too."

She grinned and joined her family.

The Brooks sisters were the last ones downstairs.

We could all hear their conversation as their boots thumped on the wooden stairway.

"I tell you, it's too late for breakfast." That was Betty Ann's voice. "We slept in."

"You set your watch wrong again, dear. The clock in our room said we're right on time."

"We won't miss the train?"

Sally Marie stopped next to the reception desk to wait for her sister. "We won't miss the train. It doesn't leave until nine o'clock. We have plenty of time."

Rose guided the ladies to the end of the buffet. "You're going on the 1880 Train this morning?"

Betty Ann looked at Rose in astonishment. "You know about the train?"

"Yes, I do. It's a popular attraction."

"You should come with us." She turned to Sally Marie. "Don't you think so, sister? Shouldn't Miss Rose come with us on the train? It would be fun."

"I already have plans for this morning." Rose's voice was friendly as well as firm. "But I know you will have a wonderful time. And there are a lot of interesting shops at both ends of the route."

Joy Albert spoke up. "We went on that train ride yesterday. We had lunch at the Alpine Inn in Hill City, and it was fabulous."

"See, Betty Ann? Let's eat breakfast right away so we can get on our way."

Once breakfast was over and cleaned up, it was time to go to town. I rolled my shoulders. Why was I dreading the interview with Anna Grace? I wasn't going to accuse her of anything. Amiable Anna Grace wasn't a criminal. At least I hoped she wasn't.

Becky met me at the reception desk. "Are you

ready?"

"Did you contact Ashley?" I said as we walked out the door.

"She's expecting us about eleven-thirty. After we talk to Anna Grace, we'll go over to Pete's to get our lunch. She said she likes his salads."

"I thought Pete's Sammiches only did sandwiches."

"Ashley said you can order a sandwich without the roll, and he'll put it in a bowl with salad greens." Becky glanced at me. "You look like you're heading to your execution. Are you still worried about talking to Anna Grace?"

"Yesterday I left her store thinking she was hiding something. I'm not sure what we'll find out when we talk to her."

We turned onto Main Street. My steps slowed as we drew closer to Living Wild.

Becky grasped my elbow. "Come on. Let's tackle this and get it over with."

She knocked on the front door. We could see Anna Grace inside, arranging items on her display shelves. She waved to us and came over to unlock the door.

"Hi. What are you two doing here so early?"

She didn't seem like she was hiding anything this morning.

I took a deep breath. "I have something to ask you. Can we talk for a few minutes?"

"Sure." She let us in, then locked the door behind us. "I hope you don't mind if I keep working while we talk. I was so busy yesterday that I have to restock before I open."

"We can help," Becky said. "What do you need us

to do?"

Anna Grace turned to a box she had just opened. "These items are next. They all need to be unpacked and dusted before I put them on the shelves."

"Perfect." Becky knelt on the floor next to the box. "We'll unpack and you can arrange the display."

I joined her on the floor and took a small box out of the shipping box and opened it. Inside, wrapped in a sheet of bubble wrap was a cute bird figurine.

Anna Grace started the conversation. "Are you still wondering about those pictures?"

The ache in my shoulders disappeared. "Yes. You said you sold them all. Do you remember who bought them?"

"Different people. I was surprised they were popular. But I still had a half-dozen left until yesterday morning."

"What happened yesterday?"

"It was the strangest thing." Anna Grace took the goldfinch figurine from me and set it on a shelf. "An older couple came in. I think they're staying at the inn. The woman is in a wheelchair."

Becky shot a glance at me.

"Violet and Charles?" I asked.

"Yes. Charles Bishop was the name on his credit card. They were waiting at the front door when I opened. They didn't look at anything else but went straight to the display of pictures and took every last one. I wrapped them up, they paid for them, and then left."

"Did they say why they bought them?"

Anna Grace shook her head. "They didn't say anything. Some customers are like that, but most will visit a bit while they make their purchase."

Becky changed the subject while we finished unpacking the box, then we left so Anna Grace could get ready for her ten o'clock store opening.

"What do you think?" she asked once we were on the sidewalk.

We stopped between Living Wild and Pete's Sammiches.

"Does it seem strange that Violet and Charles bought all the pictures she had left?" I asked.

She shrugged. "Maybe they were buying souvenirs to take home. Or gifts for relatives."

Gifts. That was probably it. Violet had said something earlier about buying gifts while they were here.

As we crossed Main Street, Cal pulled into a parking spot in front of Simon Sminski's t-shirt shop. He didn't get out of his SUV but waved us over.

"What are you two up to?"

Becky held up the bag from Pete's. "Just heading over to have lunch with Ashley."

"You're not working on the case?"

I stared into the mirrored lenses of his sunglasses. "You told us to stay out of your investigation."

"Good."

"Have you found out anything new?"

"It looks like you might have been right about Mike's death being another murder."

"Another murder? You do think Caro's death was murder now?"

He took his glasses off. "I'm working with that theory."

"What makes you think Mike was a victim?"

"A witness saw him in the alley behind the art gallery on Sunday evening, heading toward the park. He might have seen something that got him killed."

"That's awful," Becky said.

"Yup." Cal slid his sunglasses back on. "You two keep your distance, all right? I don't want anything happening to you."

"We'll try," I answered.

We continued to the sidewalk and headed toward Between the Pages. Cal's SUV passed us and pulled into an empty parking spot ahead of us. He got out and stopped us in front of the Grizzly Peak Grill, his hands on his hips.

"What did you mean, you'll try?"

Becky looked at the sidewalk somewhere around her toes. I took a step toward Cal.

"There are other lines of inquiry to follow that don't involve the art gallery. We're pursuing those. Don't worry. We'll leave the drug angle to you."

He looked from me, to Becky, and back again. "You're still chasing the nicotine connection?"

"Like you said before, I don't see a drug dealer using poison. And both Caro and Mike having a large amount of nicotine in their system is too weird to be a coincidence."

"You don't think the deaths are connected to the drugs we found?"

"I'm not sure. But since you're pursuing that angle, we thought we'd continue on this other trail."

Cal rubbed his chin. "As long as it keeps you out of trouble, go ahead."

We said goodbye and watched him drive away.

"Like he could stop us," Becky muttered.

"He could give us a direct order."

"Yeah. Right. He's been trying to order me around since we were kids. It didn't work then, and it won't work now." Becky lifted our lunch bag. "Come on. Ashley is going to start wondering where we are."

Ashley looked up when the bell tinkled.

"Hi. Come on in. We can sit at the table back here."

The bookstore was quiet, but there were a few customers. A mom with a couple children were in the picture book section and a few people were browsing through the stacks.

Becky waved to the mom and took our lunch to the table near the back door. "You don't need to take care of your customers?"

Ashley set a bell on the counter near the cash register and joined us.

"I encourage people to take their time while they're here. If someone needs help, they can ring the bell."

"How is business?" I asked as we unpacked the food.

"Pretty good." Ashley opened her salad bowl and mixed the ingredients together. "A lot of tourists have come in looking for books by local authors and information about the area. And the locals are beginning to find me." She nodded toward the mom and children. "I think she's one of your cousins, isn't she, Becky?"

"That's Tracy. She's my cousin Matt's wife. Their kids are pretty cute, aren't they?"

"Darling. This is their second time here since I opened. The children each picked out a book on their last visit. That's how to raise readers."

I took a bite of my sandwich. "This is delicious."

"Isn't it?" Ashley speared a piece of ham with her fork. "It's the dressing. Pete uses an oil and vinegar concoction of his own on the sandwiches and the salads. He won't give me the recipe."

Tracy's daughter ran over to Ashley. "I'm going to get this one. It's my favorite."

I looked at the cover. "Billy Blue Bear! He's my favorite, too."

The little girl grinned. "Do you know him?"

"I have one of his books. The author is staying at the inn this week."

Tracy had come up with her little boy in tow, "You're kidding," she said. "Debbie Walker is here in Paragon? Scout loved the first book we bought last week and had to see if there were more Billy Blue Bear books." She leaned over and swung the toddler onto her hip, "Shepherd isn't quite as excited yet. But he'll grow into them."

Scout ran back to the children's section and brought another book. She handed it to me. "Have you read this one?"

The cover showed the little bear riding a pony. "Not yet." I read the title. "'Billy Blue Bear Out West.' It looks like fun."

Ashley stood up. "Are you ready to check out?" she asked Tracy.

"I don't want to interrupt your lunch."

"Not a problem." She led the way to the cash register, Scout skipping beside her.

I leafed through the book in my hands, smiling at the illustrations. In the back was a photo of Debbie and a short biography.

"This is interesting."

"What?" Becky asked.

I handed her the book, open to Debbie's bio. "Look where she went to school."

She read the line I was pointing to, then locked her gaze on mine. "The same school Caro attended."

I tapped the date. "And she graduated a year later. This proves it was Debbie in the photo. They had to have known each other."

Ashley joined us again. "I can't believe Debbie Walker is in town. If I had known she was coming, we could have scheduled a book signing. But maybe she'll stop by and sign the copies I have on the shelf. Do you think she would?"

"I have no idea. But she and her husband are here until Saturday, so maybe. You'll have to ask her."

"Will she be there tonight? I could come up after I close the store."

Becky had finished her sandwich. "You might miss her. The guests are often away until later at night. You could catch her at breakfast, though. Why don't you come tomorrow morning around seven? We'll have breakfast together and introduce you." She turned to me. "And we can ask her if she knew Caro."

"Caro Lewis?" Ashley's eyes grew round. "The art gallery owner who died?" Her eyes narrowed and her voice dropped. "I heard she might have been murdered. Are you two investigating?"

I glanced around to see if any of the remaining customers had heard her, but they were still engrossed in the books at the front of the store.

"We're following leads, but nothing definite." I finished my sandwich.

"Maybe you could help us," Becky said.

"Oh, I'd love to!"

I tried to give Becky a warning shake of my head, but she ignored me. I resigned myself to sharing the clues with another amateur sleuth. First Taylor and now Ashley. Pretty soon the whole town would be in on the action.

Becky leaned closer to the bookstore owner. "Your shop is right across the street from the art gallery. Have you seen anything suspicious?"

Ashley shook her head slowly. "Not that I can think of." She frowned. "Wait. I saw lights over there the other night. Sunday night. I live upstairs, above the store, and I was looking out at the stars before I went to bed. That's when I saw the lights in Caro's building. I thought there might be a vacation rental on her second floor. A lot of the buildings have them, you know."

"There isn't one at the art gallery that I know of." I reviewed the building's layout in my mind. The only stairs to the second floor were on the photo shop side of the building, the ones Cal said went to Tyrone Jackson's apartment, but no one had seen him yet this season. "You're sure the lights were on the second floor and not the ground floor?"

"Absolutely." Ashley nodded. "There are curtains or blinds covering the windows, but the lights were on."

"Did you see them any other night?"

"No. Only Sunday."

Becky and I exchanged glances. It was definitely something to tell Cal about.

One of the customers had heard our conversation. The man held an open book in his hands, but he was watching us. It was time to change the subject.

"How long have you lived in Paragon, Ashley?"

"Almost a month. But the area isn't new to me. I grew up in Rapid City."

Becky leaned her elbows on the table. "You lived in Rapid, but decided to open your bookstore in Paragon?"

Ashley laughed. "I know. It seems like I'd have more traffic in the city, right? But I've always wanted to live in the Hills, so when I received an inheritance from my granny, I used it to pursue my dream. She had always encouraged me to open my own bookstore. I did my research and chose Paragon. This little town has a lot of traffic, both during the season and in the winter."

"And you mentioned on-line sales, too?" I asked.

She nodded. "That's the biggest part of my business. I've had an on-line store for a couple years. Opening a brick-and-mortar shop was the next step."

"You've made it a welcoming place. I'd spend a day browsing here any time." I glanced again at the man who had been listening to us, but he had moved to a different stack of shelves. "You'll have to look at the library at the inn when you're there tomorrow. Rose has an interesting collection of books, including some first edition Agatha Christies."

Ashley put her fork down. "Really?"

I nodded. "Most of them are signed."

"How did she get such treasures?"

"You won't believe it. She met Agatha Christie years ago and bought the copies then."

"I hope she has a good security system. They could be worth a small fortune."

"Don't worry. She does." My phone alarm buzzed. "That's the signal to get back to work."

Becky gathered up the empty wrappers from our

sandwiches. "We'll have to do this again sometime."

"You're right." Ashley added her salad bowl to the bag of trash and tossed it in a nearby waste basket. "In the fall I'll have more free time, but until then you're welcome to have lunch here any time. I'm glad to get to know both of you better."

Becky and I left the store, the bell tinkling overhead on our way out.

"That was fun," I said. "With Ashley we make a pretty good threesome. Like the three musketeers."

"Or like a S'more."

"A S'more?"

"You know, the campfire treat. Marshmallows, chocolate, and graham crackers. The three things together, like the three of us. A S'more just isn't a S'more without all three."

I laughed. "Okay. I think I know what you mean."

We crossed the highway and walked up Graves' Gulch Road.

"What's next in the investigation?" asked Becky.

We had reached the inn. The parking lot was empty, which told me all the guests were still away for the day. "I'm curious about what Debbie might know about Caro. If they went to school together, why hasn't she mentioned it before?"

Becky stopped on the front porch. "You don't think she's the murderer, do you?"

"I don't know. I hate to think so, but-"

"But you found the nicotine spray in Rick and Debbie's room." Becky's face was grim. "They could be in it together."

"I need to ask Debbie about Caro. I don't think she's the killer, but she might know something about Caro that could lead us in the right direction."

Becky opened the inn's front door. "You mean you hope she's not the killer."

Debbie Walker a murderer? I pushed that idea away as I went to the utility room to grab the vacuum. A person who wrote sweet children's books couldn't be a killer.

Thirteen

The guests returned to the inn for tea one group at a time. The Brooks sisters were first.

"Oh, Emma!" Betty Ann planted herself between me and the buffet counter. "You won't guess what we did this afternoon."

I moved around her to set the tray of sweeteners next to the pitcher of iced tea. "You'll have to tell me."

"We saw real buffalo!" She took Sally Marie's arm. "Tell her about the buffalo."

"She's right." Sally Marie nodded her head with enthusiasm. "We went on a guided tour at Custer State Park, and the driver took us everywhere. He knew right where to find the herd of buffalo. There were hundreds of them."

"With their babies. They were so cute that I wanted to take one home, but Sally Marie said we couldn't."

"The tour guide said we couldn't. But we did the next best thing." Sally Marie opened her shopping bag and pulled out a toy buffalo. "We bought the biggest one the store had. Now we can take our buffalo home."

"His name is Custer," Betty Ann said as she took the toy from her sister and hugged it. "We'll put it with our other souvenirs from this trip."

"What other souvenirs have you found?" I asked.

Sally Marie peered into her shopping bag. "Some coffee mugs with a picture of Mount Rushmore on them, and sweatshirts to wear this winter."

"Don't forget the things we bought in Paragon the other day." Betty Ann tugged on Sally Marie's sleeve.

"That's right. We found some cute little birds in one of the stores in town."

Just then, Rick and Debbie came in along with Dave and Joy. "Excuse me. I need to ask Debbie something."

As I walked toward the reception desk, I heard Betty Ann say, "You didn't tell her about the pictures."

"That's all right, dear. Let's have some tea."

I made a mental note to ask the ladies what pictures they meant, then greeted the two couples.

"Did you have a good day of sight-seeing?"

"It was splendid," Joy said. "We went to Deadwood and did their historical walking tour. So interesting!"

"And after the walking tour we did some shopping," Debbie said as she held up a bag. "It was a great town to visit."

The front door opened again, and the Thomas family came in led by Toni. Before Debbie moved on to the tea buffet, I touched her elbow to get her attention.

"Could I talk to you for a few minutes after tea?"

Her answering smile was warm. "Of course."

Taylor and Toni stopped to greet me as Debbie went on to the dining room.

"Have you ever been in a cave?" Toni asked.

"Is that what you did today?"

Toni hopped on one foot. "Uh huh. It was spooky when they turned the lights out."

"You wouldn't believe how dark it was," Taylor said. "There was no light at all! But the rest of the tour was beautiful. I never knew there could be so many cool things underground."

"I'll have to try it some time."

As the rest of the family went into the dining room, Taylor hung back. "Dad wants to go to some rodeo tonight, so I won't be able to help you and Becky."

"Don't worry about it. We don't have many new clues to work with anyway. The rodeo will be a lot more fun."

Rose came in with Thatcher and joined me at the reception desk.

"It's good to see everyone enjoying themselves," she said.

I gave Thatcher a pat. "You know you spoil your guests."

"What do you mean?"

"I don't know of any other B&B that serves afternoon tea."

She laughed. "It gives a unique touch to the Sweetbrier, doesn't it? And look how the guests form friendships during the time they're here."

"Do any of the friendships last more than a week?"

"There are a three couples who met the first year we were open. One couple is from Washington, another from Minnesota, and the third from New Mexico. They'll all be here the last week of June for their annual reunion."

"Do you think the Walkers and the Alberts will do the same thing?" I nodded toward the two couples who were chatting together at one of the tables.

"I wouldn't be surprised."

A few minutes later, Debbie caught my eye, and I joined her at her table as the others went upstairs.

"You wanted to ask me something?" she asked.

I glanced at the guests remaining in the dining room. "Can we go someplace quieter?"

She followed me into the library and we each sat in one of the comfortable armchairs.

"Becky and I had lunch with Ashley at the bookstore today, and your name came up." I smiled. "One of her young customers loves your books. Ashley is going to ask if you might stop by and sign a few copies that are in the store."

"It would be my pleasure." Then a slight frown crossed her face. "But that isn't all you wanted to discuss, is it?"

I leaned forward. "I read in your biography that you graduated from Forestgreen Academy of Art. Did you know Caro Lewis when you were there?"

Debbie sighed. "I wondered if anyone would make that connection. We were at the school together."

"You graduated the year after her, right?"

She nodded. "We were involved in different programs. I took the design and illustration track, and Caro was in painting. She was only interested in contemporary art."

I brought up the photo of Caro with the painting on my phone. "Does this picture look familiar?"

Debbie took the phone from me and looked at it closer. "Yes. This was used as a publicity picture for the academy for a few years." She pointed to the left edge of the photo. "That's Caro, there."

"And the painting?"

"It isn't finished in this photo, but that's the painting that won the Highspring Award. It was displayed in the academy's museum and gained international recognition. I wonder what happened to it."

"It's in the art gallery here in Paragon."

"Caro's gallery? That makes sense. It was her one great success. Nothing she painted since then came close to the genius of this painting."

I swept my finger over the screen to show her the next picture. "Do you recognize this one?"

"That was one of our many trips to the Chicago Art Institute." She pointed. "There I am. My, that was a long time ago."

"And that's Caro, right?" I enlarged the picture so Caro was in the center. "Who is next to her?"

"That's Letty Carmichael. Now that's a tragic story." Debbie took the phone from me and gazed at the photo. "She and Caro were best friends, but also fierce competitors. Letty was the more talented, but Caro was tenacious."

"What did they compete over?"

"Everything. Grades, honors, awards, the best location in an exhibit. It didn't matter what it was."

"What happened?"

"Only a few weeks before they were supposed to graduate, Letty was in a car accident. She was in the hospital for a long time. When I came back to school in the fall, I heard she had been in a coma all summer and wasn't expected to survive." Debbie shook her head. "Such a loss. She had incredible talent."

I scrolled back to the first picture. "This person on the right-hand side of the picture. Who is she?"

"That's Letty. In fact, that picture was taken the day before the accident that claimed her life."

"She's almost completely cut out of this photo. How can you be sure it's her?"

"There's a much better copy of this photo on the academy's website. Where did you find this one?"

"It was included with Caro's biography on the same website. I'll have to look further."

"It should be with the pictures from that class's graduating year. It would have been nineteen seventy-two."

I put my phone back in my pocket. "Thank you for talking with me. You've been a great help."

"Why did you want to know about Caro?"

"I'm helping the police with their investigation into her death. When I saw you went to the same school, I thought you might provide some helpful background."

"I'm not sure how much help I've been. We didn't travel in the same circles at school."

"You weren't friends, then."

"Oh, no." She gave a slight shudder. "I don't mind telling you, since you want to know about Caro, she didn't like me at all. We would call her a bully today, but back then she was a pain in the neck. I went out of my way to avoid her."

"She bullied you?"

Debbie grimaced. "I was her target. I was shy, which she thought was a sign of weakness. And my illustrations weren't up to her standards of art. She made my life miserable, belittling me every chance she got, and she even sabotaged my art supplies. I don't know how many times I found my pen nibs broken or my inks mixed together. I could never prove it was her, though. My senior year should have been better, but after she graduated, she remained at the school as an adjunct professor. I'm glad I never had to take any of her classes."

I took a deep breath. Debbie certainly had a motive to lash out at Caro. "Are you happy she's dead?"

Her eyes widened. "No, of course not. I hadn't seen her since I graduated, and I've put all that behind me. It's tragic she died in that way - alone. I understand it was a heart attack?"

"Yes. Does that surprise you?"

"The only surprise is that it didn't happen sooner. Everyone at school knew about her heart condition. She often predicted she would die a tragic death at a young age." Debbie laid the back of her hand against her forehead in a melodramatic gesture. "Giving her life to her art." She abandoned the pose with a sad smile. "I guess she got her wish."

After supper, Becky and I met in my suite with my computer. I opened the academy's website.

"Debbie said we would find an uncropped photo on another page."

I found Caro's graduating year and clicked on the link. I scrolled down.

"There it is," Becky said.

Tim was perched on the couch behind her, and Thatcher was snuggled between us. Both animals were watching with interest.

I clicked on the photo and it filled the screen.

Debbie had been right. We could see the entire picture. Caro and Letty stood on either side of the large unfinished painting while several other students gathered around them.

"It must be the whole graduating class. And that," I pointed to the figure on the right, "is Letty Carmichael, according to Debbie." I related Letty's story to Becky.

"That's too bad. She still looks like Violet Bishop, but it can't be her. I wonder if they were related."

"That's an interesting idea. Let's do a search for Letty. There should be an obituary and they usually list surviving family members."

I typed in the name and clicked enter.

Suddenly a strident voice came from the lounge outside my door, calling my name.

"Emma! Emma! Come quick!"

Thatcher ran to the door with his alarm bark. Betty Ann was making her way through the lounge from her room.

I ran to her and took her arm. "What is it? What's wrong?"

"Sally Marie. Something is wrong with her." Betty Ann twisted to point back to the open door of her room. Her sister was collapsed on the floor.

Becky brushed past me. "I'll get Rose."

I knelt next to Sally Marie, my stomach clutching when I saw her ashen face. I felt for a pulse. It was weak, but it was there.

"What happened?"

"She was getting ready for bed, then she said she didn't feel good and fell to the floor." Betty Ann's tears streamed down her face. "Oh, my poor sister. What can we do?"

Rose rushed up, followed by Becky. "What do you think, Emma? Does she need medical help?"

"Definitely. Her breathing is shallow and she's not responding." I loosened the top button of Sally Marie's pajama top and tried to move her to a position that would make breathing easier, but her bulk made it impossible.

Becky pulled out her phone. "I'll call 911."

While we waited, Rose tried to calm Betty Ann while I pulled the blanket off the bed to cover Sally Marie. Something that had been tangled in the folds fell to the floor. I reached to pick it up but snatched my hand back. It was one of the pictures from Anna Grace's store.

Cal arrived within minutes after Becky called him, followed by the ambulance. I heard him take the stairs two at a time, then he was moving people away from Sally Marie's inert form. Rose and I took Betty Ann to the lounge outside their door, then I slipped back in. Cal had put an oxygen mask over Sally Marie's nose and mouth, and she was awake. She gave me a weak wave of her fingers.

I waved back. "Do you need any help?" I asked Cal.

He had been listening to Sally Marie's heart and lungs with a stethoscope, but then finished and turned to me. "It looks like she's going to be fine." He had clipped an oximeter to her finger and checked the readout. "Her heartbeat is good, and her oxygen levels are back to normal.

I turned and gave Rose a thumbs up.

"Did you notice-"

He held up the picture sealed in an evidence bag. "Yup. First thing." He stashed his medical supplies in his bag and stood up. "Sally Marie, let's see if we can get you back into bed. Do you feel like sitting up?"

She snatched the oxygen mask from her face. "I certainly do. It feels funny to be lying on the floor like this."

Cal motioned to the EMTs from the ambulance and they sat her up. While she rested in that position for a minute, Betty Ann peered in the door.

"Sally Marie! You aren't dead!"

"Why would I be dead?" Cal and the other EMTs helped her onto the bed. "I was a little swoony, but I'm fine now."

Betty Ann sat next to her. "Are you sure? You don't need the hospital?"

Her sister shook her head. "I'm fine. This nice deputy said I was. It's time to stop making such a fuss."

I took her cue and joined the group in the lounge outside their room. The Walkers and the Alberts had joined the others in the lounge and Cal and Rose came out of the Dublin Bay. The EMTs conferred with Cal for a few minutes, then they left.

Cal joined the waiting group, the picture in his gloved hand.

"Does anyone else have one of these pictures they purchased from Living Wild in town?" he asked.

"We do," said Rick.

Dave and Joy nodded. "We bought one, too. We thought it would be a great souvenir of our trip."

"I would like to see them. We've had a rash of poisonings in town over the last few days, and they all seem to be connected to these pictures."

"Sally Marie was poisoned?" Rick asked. "With what?"

"I'll have to test her picture to tell for sure. I'd like to test yours, also."

"I'll get ours," Debbie said. She and Joy both turned toward their rooms.

Cal called after them. "Be sure to wrap them in a towel or something. Don't touch them with your bare skin."

Both women went into their rooms. Debbie was the first one out, but her hands were empty.

"It isn't here," she said. "Rick, did you put it away?"

At that moment, Joy came out of her room. "It's gone. I thought it was on my bedside table."

Dave shrugged. "I didn't do anything with it."

Cal glanced at me, and I tilted my head toward my suite. This needed to be discussed in private.

"Let me know if you find them," Cal said. "And since everything is fine with Sally Marie, you can all go about your business. We'll let her rest and I'll check on her again before I leave."

As the Alberts and the Walkers continued on their way to supper, Cal and Becky joined me in my living room. Thatcher ran in as I was closing the door.

"I know I saw those pictures when I cleaned the other day," I said.

"In those two rooms?"

Cal held the plastic wrapped picture out of reach as Thatcher strained his nose toward it.

"Let him smell it," I said. "You never know what he might find out."

"How is he going to tell us?" Cal frowned but

lowered the picture for Thatcher.

The corgi took one sniff, then whined and backed away. He looked at me and gave a wag of his tail. Where had I seen him do that before?

Mike. It was after he sniffed Mike's fingers in the cemetery.

"I think he smells the nicotine." I took the picture from Cal and held it close to Thatcher again. "Is that it, buddy? Is it like what you smelled on Mike's fingers?"

Thatcher backed up and put a paw over his nose.

"I told you that dog was smart," Becky said, giving him a rub behind the ears. "He can tell us where the nicotine is."

"But that doesn't tell us if the pictures were intentionally poisoned, or if it was something that happened in the factory."

I leaned against the back of the sectional. "What evidence would you need that someone intentionally dosed them with nicotine in order to kill Caro?"

Cal took a toothpick out of his pocket. "We would need actual nicotine, plus a motive."

Becky nodded. "Means, motive, and opportunity, right?"

My stomach flipped. I knew someone who had all three. I went to the crime board and started a new list.

"Means," I said aloud as I wrote the word. "Could it be a concentrated solution of nicotine? Like in a nasal spray designed to help people stop smoking?"

"What kind of concentrate are we talking about?"

Cal looked interested enough for me to continue.

"I can look it up." I opened my computer and searched for the product I had seen in the Walker's room. "Would one hundred milligrams be enough?"

"Let me check my notes." Cal pulled a small notebook out of his back pocket and flipped a few pages. "More than enough. Fifty is a fatal dose."

"Then they would only need half of the bottle." I wrote on the board.

"Don't forget the lab said there wasn't enough nicotine to kill most people. Just enough to make them sick," Becky said.

We looked at each other.

"Like Sally Marie." Becky's voice trembled.

I erased what I had written. The killer would need less than fifty milligrams.

"What motive do you have?" Cal asked. "The drugs?"

"That could be one." I wrote it on the board. "But maybe the person didn't like Caro for some reason."

I wrote that on the board, too, thinking of what Debbie had told me about her relationship with Caro. Every word I wrote felt like I was stabbing her in the back.

"What about the opportunity?" Becky asked.

"I don't have that answer." I put the cap back on the marker, relieved. I could create a scenario where Debbie could poison the pictures, but that wouldn't be a real clue.

"Anyone could have gone to Living Wild and swiped the poison onto the picture frames while they were pretending to be shopping," Cal said.

"You're speculating?" I asked. "That isn't like you."

"Just talking through the clues." He shrugged. "It seems to work for you and Becky." He read through the notes on the board. "So, Emma, who fits your profile? Who had the means, motive, and opportunity?"

I clamped my mouth closed. I didn't want to mention Debbie's name until I was certain.

"It has to be Debbie, right?" Becky pointed to the motive I had written on the board. "She's the only one who fits that motive."

Cal chewed on his toothpick. "Debbie and Caro went to the same school?"

"That's right." Becky said. "We have a photo from the school with both of them in it."

"What about the means?" Cal looked at me. "Where did you find the bottle of nasal spray?"

"In the Walker's room." I capped the marker and set it in the tray. "It looks like Debbie is the murderer."

Cal shook his head. "Don't jump to conclusions. Do you have any evidence?"

"I found the bottle of nasal spray in Debbie's room."

"Was it empty?"

I shook my head.

"That bottle might not have been the source of the nicotine."

I felt hope growing.

"That doesn't get her off the hook, though. She could have several bottles. What about her motive? When she talked about Caro, did she sound bitter or angry?"

"No. She admitted they hadn't been friends at school, but she kind of laughed it off. Said it was a long time ago."

Becky gave my arm a gentle punch. "See? It wasn't Debbie." She looked as relieved as I felt.

"I didn't say that," said Cal. "I'm only pointing out

that even though you could look at these clues and draw the conclusion that she's the murderer, it isn't the only solution. She had means, motive, and opportunity, but many other people could also have had those three things."

"Or it might not have been done on purpose at all." Becky sprawled on the couch. "Which leaves us with no murder."

"Which is what I've been saying all along." Cal smiled smugly.

"But that doesn't change the fact that two people are dead." I pushed Becky's feet off the couch and sat next to her. "If they weren't murdered-"

"Both deaths could have been unfortunate accidents." Cal sat on the short L of the sectional and rested his feet on the ottoman.

I studied the clue board as Thatcher climbed onto the couch next to me. Tim, on his perch next to my head, purred like a buzz saw.

"What about the drug angle?" I turned to Cal. "Have you made any progress there?"

"Not as much as I'd like. And I'm beginning to wonder where Tyrone Jackson is."

"He still hasn't opened his shop?" Becky asked. "He's always here by Memorial Day weekend." She sat up. "You don't think the same person who did Caro in got to him, too?"

I looked from Becky to Cal. "Didn't someone say he lives on the second floor of the old school building? Ashley said she saw lights there the other night."

Cal rubbed his chin, then checked his watch. "It's getting late. I need to check on Sally Marie, and then I'll go home. I'll keep an eye on the art gallery tonight, though. If someone is using Tyrone's apartment, they might be involved in the drug ring, too."

"What if you don't see any activity?" I asked. "Will you investigate further?"

"I'll check the place out in the morning. Something fishy is going on."

"Can I go with you?" I sat up and leaned toward Cal. "I'd like to see this through to the end."

"I told you following the drug trail could be dangerous."

"But if you don't see anyone around tonight or in the morning, then it would be safe, right?" I nudged the toe of his boot that still rested on my ottoman. "And you said two sets of eyes are better than one."

Cal rose to his feet. "All right. I'll call you around nine if I need you." He strode to the door and picked up his bag. "But-"

"I know." I followed him and opened the door. "I'll be careful."

He paused, his brown eyes searching mine. His chin dipped as his eyes dropped to my mouth, then his gaze shifted to Becky who was watching and listening from her spot on the couch.

"I'll be counting on it." His voice was low and growly.

I closed the door as he went across the lounge toward the Dublin Bay.

"Well," said Becky. "That was interesting."

I pushed the memory of Cal's gentle concern to the back of my mind. "What was?"

"That little goodbye scene. What would have happened if I hadn't been here?"

I touched my lips, resting my fingers on the soft surface. What would have happened?

Fourteen

The fragrance of frying bacon pulled me into the kitchen the next morning.

"Hey, girl. Are you ready for your coffee?"

Becky was all sunshine and roses, even as early as it was. I grinned back at her. I could do sunshine and roses, too.

"Sure thing."

She poured a cup for each of us, then leaned on the prep counter, watching me.

"So..." She let the word linger as she stirred cream into her coffee. "How did you sleep last night?"

"Good." I inhaled the caffeine-laden steam from my own cup. "I always sleep well in the mountains. Why?"

"Oh, I thought a certain someone might be on your mind."

I let my mind play over the way Cal had left me the evening before until I saw Becky watching me with a satisfied grin.

"What?"

"Just you two. I knew you and Cal would get together eventually."

"We're not together."

"Oh yeah? Then what was that look that passed between you if it wasn't an 'I can't wait to be alone with you' look."

I laughed. "You read a lot more into that look than was actually there."

"I don't think so." She sipped her coffee, studying me. "You're serious, aren't you? You don't think there's anything going on between you and Cal."

"There isn't." There wasn't. "It's all in your imagination."

"Sure. Whatever you say."

I was desperate to change the subject. "That bacon smells wonderful. What are you fixing for breakfast this morning?"

It worked. Becky was all about the food. "We're having bacon, egg, and cheese croissant sandwiches and grilled asparagus."

"Asparagus for breakfast?"

"Sure? Why not? The asparagus patch in the garden is growing like crazy. What better way to use it than serve it with breakfast? And the strawberries in the greenhouse are ready to pick. I tossed them with some mint leaves from the herb garden and a light sweet glaze for our breakfast fruit."

"I'm impressed that so much has come from our own garden already. It's only beginning to grow, isn't it?"

Becky nodded. "While you've been out chasing bad guys, Rose and I have been discussing what to plant this year. We might add some chickens, too. They will give us fresh eggs for the season."

"That's about as local as you can get." I checked the clock on the wall. "It's time to get the dining room ready."

Becky had turned to take the sheet pan of bacon out of the oven. "Ashley texted me last night. She'll have breakfast with us." She set the pan on the counter. "And don't forget Cal said he'd call this morning."

I let the kitchen door swing closed behind me.

The Brooks sisters were the first ones to breakfast, clomping down the steps at seven o'clock on the dot.

"How are you ladies this morning?" I watched Sally Marie closely but didn't see any ill effects from the events of last night.

"I'm fine," Betty Ann said, "but Sally Marie is more like a garden snail than a June bug this morning."

"I am not." Sally Marie pulled her elbow out of her sister's grasp. "I'm as right as rain. Stop fussing over me."

"I thought you were going to die."

Sally Marie stalked over to the coffee maker. "But I didn't. I'm fine."

She poured herself a cup of coffee and grabbed three blue packets before heading to a table while Betty Ann watched with a worried frown on her face.

"Maybe we should stay here and rest this morning."

"And miss the fossils? Don't be silly." Sally Marie shook the blue packets before opening them. "I want to watch the workers dig, just like the brochure said."

Betty Ann turned to Rose, who had returned from walking Thatcher. "Don't you think she should stay home and rest?"

"I think she should listen to her own body. Deputy Cal said she was fine, so if she feels like going sight-seeing today, then she probably can. You won't be doing anything too strenuous, will you?"

"We're going to the Mammoth Site in Hot Springs. From the brochure, it looks like it's all indoors with a short walk around the dig."

"I wouldn't worry, then. Just let Sally Marie set the pace and rest if she gets tired."

Ashley came in a few minutes after the Walkers came down for their breakfast, and I introduced them.

"You own a bookstore?" Debbie asked. "How wonderful. I need to stop in and see it." She laid a hand on Ashley's arm. "I have to warn you, Rick will need to drag me out of there. I lose all track of time when I'm browsing."

Ashley laughed, as captivated by Debbie's manner as I was. "I hope you'll take a few minutes to autograph the copies of your books I have in my children's section."

"I would love to! And I hope a couple of your young customers will be there. I always enjoy talking with children about their favorite books."

By the time breakfast was over and the guests had left for their daily plans and Ashley had gone back to her store, Cal still hadn't called. As I loaded the dishwasher, Becky took another batch of hamburger buns out of the oven.

"You don't think he forgot, do you?"

"Who?" I filled the detergent dispenser and closed the dishwasher's door.

"Cal. Didn't he say he'd call around nine? It's after nine now."

It was nine twenty-five. "I don't think we need to worry. He said he might call if he needed me."

Becky dumped a bowl full of bread dough on the counter. "He should call anyway, if he cared about you."

I watched her pinch pieces of dough off the lump and roll them into balls. "There isn't any romance happening between us. We're just-"

The kitchen door swung open, and Cal stood in the doorway.

"We're just what?" he said.

I gave Becky what I meant to be a withering look. How much of our conversation had he heard?

"We're going to try to figure out what's going on with the guy that runs the Old Time Photo shop."

It was lame, but it got us past the embarrassing moment.

"Tyrone Jackson," Cal said. "I didn't see anything suspicious when I made my rounds last night so I'm going to see if I can figure out what's going on." He patted his breast pocket. "I've obtained a warrant, so we're set to go."

I punched the start button on the dishwasher and followed Cal out to his SUV.

"Don't you need a compelling reason to get a warrant?" I asked as I fastened my seat belt and Cal backed out of the driveway.

"Yes, but I did a bit of investigating last night, following Tyrone's trail. He left New Mexico at the end of April, when he usually does. He is normally in Paragon by mid-May. I was able to track credit card purchases as he traveled north, but the trail disappeared in Colorado."

"What do you mean? Has something happened to him?"

"Maybe. His last credit card purchase was in

Pueblo, Colorado on May fifth. Between that and Caro's death, the judge agreed to the warrant."

"He could have stopped using credit and paid with cash." I tried to imagine Tyrone's route from Arizona to the Black Hills. "Even so, he should be here by now, right?"

"He should be." As he pulled to a stop in the alley behind the old school building, he brought up a picture on his SUV's computer and turned the screen toward me. "Here's what he looks like, in case you happen to see him around town."

The man had a pleasant enough face and looked like he was in his mid-fifties. His most noticeable feature was an old-style handlebar mustache.

"I think I'd recognize him with no problem if he still has that mustache."

"He probably does. It's a trademark for his photo business. He looks the part of a shopkeeper from the eighteen-hundreds."

When we went into the photo shop's back room, I expected it to look completely different, but even though the space had been cleared of any traces of drugs by the police, it looked the same as the last time I had been here. The room was dim, and Cal pulled his flashlight from his belt and turned it on.

"We'll check upstairs first, then the front of the store."

He led the way to the stairs and started up the worn wooden treads. I tried to imagine what this building had been like in the days when it was full of the children of Paragon going up and down these stairs every day.

At the top, the stairway opened into a multi-purpose room. A couch and chair filled the space in the center, while in the back corner was a small kitchen with apartment-sized appliances. On the opposite wall was a closed door, probably leading to a bedroom. The air was stale and close. I opened the refrigerator. Four cans out of a six-pack of beer and a pizza box filled the small space. The stove top was grimy. Whoever had been here wasn't a cook.

Cal started toward the bedroom door, but then the radio on his belt let out a beeping alarm. He pushed a button and listened to the message.

"There's been a bad accident on Highway 16." He looked at me. "I have to go. Can you let yourself out?"

"Sure."

I don't think he even heard my answer as he brushed past me and ran down the stairs. I turned to follow him, but then stopped. Had I heard a sound from behind that closed door?

Cal had taken the warrant with him, so at this point, I was trespassing. I listened, but didn't hear anything other than Cal's siren speeding down the road away from Paragon. I continued down the steps.

When I reached the back room again curiosity took hold. A heavy curtain hung in the doorway between the back room and the front of the photo shop. I could peek in, just to see if anyone had been in that part of the building recently.

I moved the curtain aside and stepped through. Muted sunlight filtering through the newspaper covered windows illuminated the racks of clothes that stood on either side of the center aisle. I walked past a couple dressing rooms and pulled back the sheet that covered one of the clothing racks. It was filled with costumes. Everything from the gaudy dresses a dance hall girl would wear to the vests and skirts of a cowgirl. The next rack held men's historical costumes. A display of guns on the wall startled me until I realized they were also props. The front of the room was set up with a wild west themed backdrop. The old-time photo studio was still in winter storage.

On the wall opposite the backdrop was a counter. A message light was blinking on the old-style push button telephone. I'd let Cal know the next time I talked to him. The messages recorded on the phone might give him some clues about Tyrone's whereabouts.

Partially obscured by a curtain on the wall behind the desk was a latch, like you would see on a closet door, recessed into the panel. I pulled the curtain back and turned the latch. The door swung open into Caro's art gallery.

We had wondered if the two shops were connected, and here was the proof. The small door didn't go all the way to the floor. The opening was only a couple feet wide and about four feet high. I stepped through and let the panel close behind me.

From the art gallery side, I wouldn't have known it was there. Wallpaper extended beyond the edge of the panel, obscuring the door. Even the latch was hidden by the chair rail that had been placed at the right height. In order to open the door from this side, I needed to move a small section of the rail aside to access the latch.

Clever.

My quick look at the photo shop had taken longer than I had anticipated, and I needed to get out of the building. But before heading back through the panel, I glanced at the painting on the wall next to it. Caro's prize-winning piece.

It wasn't to my taste, I preferred the realism of the nineteenth century, but I could see why it had won the acclaim it had. The composition was balanced, and the colors flowed from one to the next in a way that suggested the movement of water. Or a spring breeze, which would be fitting with the title of the painting.

I read the plaque on the frame again, *Almost Spring*, then I stepped around the desk to look at it from a distance. There were a few differences between it and the photo we had seen on the school's website. I had saved the photo to my phone and brought it up to compare them. Something didn't look right.

I stepped over to the wall and flicked on the switch. Spotlights in the ceiling shone on the painting. The version on the wall had a different color scheme than the one on my phone. Green was the dominant color of the finished work, while the picture from the school's website was a blend of pink and lavender. Caro must have continued working on the painting after the picture was taken.

A noise from the photo shop sent a shot of panic through me. Someone was over there. I slipped to the light switch and eased it to the off position, then slowly, and I hoped silently, I eased the panel door closed. The loud click as it latched made me cringe. Footsteps approached the door.

I ran to the only cover I could see, one of the light fabric curtains that hung between the displays. As the panel door opened with a slight creak, I looked down. The curtain's bottom edge was two feet above the floor. Anyone looking in that direction would see me.

A flashlight beam traveled around the room.

"Who's there?" Heavy footsteps walked to the backroom. "Sean, are you in here?"

I took advantage of the man's attention on the other room to step to the side and crouch in between two podiums supporting Cal's cousin's sculptures. He walked back past the desk to the panel door. I peeked out, then froze. He had paused with one foot through the opening and had turned back to sweep the gallery with the flashlight beam again. I pulled back into the shadows before the light revealed my hiding place.

But I had seen the man's face. Tyrone Jackson was in town after all.

My legs were growing stiff in my crouched position. I shifted as quietly as I could, waiting for Tyrone to go back into the photo studio and close the door, but instead he came back into the gallery.

"Sean?"

This time an answer came from the back room.

"Keep it down, will you?"

Tyrone stepped back into the gallery and stood where I could see his face again. The angle of his jaw was tight, lifted in defiance.

"There's no one here but us. You heard the cop leave as well as I did."

"Anyone walking by on the street could hear you shout like that."

Tyrone scowled. I suddenly realized if I could see him, he could see me. I moved farther back into the shadows.

"We need to get out of here. It's time to leave town."

"You want out?" Sean stalked into the gallery, each

footstep heavy and deliberate. "I'm waiting for the last shipment."

Tyrone took a step back. "I'm only saying it's risky with that cop nosing around."

Another deliberate step. "I don't know why I keep you around. I should have gotten rid of you after you botched the last shipment. Cops were crawling all over this place."

"I didn't botch that. You were the one who dropped the box and scattered the profits all over the place. Besides, you need me." Tyrone's voice blustered. "I'm the connection to Caro and her shipments. Without me, you'd have nothing."

A pause. I risked a peek. Sean leaned on the desk, his sinewy body lounging cat-like as he fiddled with something in his right hand. Probably twenty years younger than Tyrone, his stance looked relaxed, but there was a hard glint to his eyes that sent a sinking feeling through my stomach.

"Don't push me, old man. You know what happened to Caro. As soon as that last shipment arrives tomorrow, I'm out of here."

Tyrone grunted. "Don't try to pull that bluff on me. Neither one of us had anything to do with Caro. She just died."

"You think so? You think Caro just..." Sean tossed the trinket into the air and caught it again. "...died?"

I pulled back again. The trinket was a knife.

"I didn't mean it that way." Tyrone's voice had changed to a frightened whine. I didn't blame him. I'd want to placate Sean, too. "I'm with you to the end, you know that. I only meant we need to get out of town as soon as we can."

"You know the drill. I take the stuff and sell it to

my contact, then I'll come back here and give you your cut."

"I don't like it."

Sean barked out a laugh. "You've made it worse for yourself, keeping your store closed. You should have opened it on time, then no one would be suspicious." Sean took another step toward Tyrone, his boot ringing on the wood floor. "Play it out like we planned, or you'll be sorry."

Another pause. I peeked out. Tyrone had gone back through the panel door to the photo shop and closed it behind him. Sean chuckled, thrust his knife into his boot, then turned and strode into the gallery's back room.

I sat on the floor, my knees shaking. That was close. Too close. If Cal knew, he'd call me on the carpet. But I couldn't keep this from him. I had to tell him what I had overheard.

But first I had to get out of here.

I listened but didn't hear any movement from the back room of the gallery. Had Sean left?

I got to my feet and crept toward the doorway, ready to dive for cover. I peered into the room. No one was there. In the corner, on the wall the two businesses shared, was a door I hadn't seen before. The large cabinet that had been in front of it had been pulled away and revealed a second door to the basement stairway. It must be where Sean had gone.

The back door leading to the alley was propped open and an open panel van was parked just beyond it. Sean emerged from the basement, carrying a box, and went out to the van. I ducked back as he turned to come back inside, but he didn't hesitate. He went back down the stairs.

This was my chance. I ran to the back door and eased outside. I walked quickly to the end of the alley and turned toward Gran's Café. Once I was at the corner, I turned to look back. The old school building stood as silent as it had ever been. No one had followed me.

Heading back to the inn, I checked my phone. Not even lunchtime yet. That whole adventure...or fiasco...had taken a little over an hour.

The inn was quiet when I got back. I knew Rose would be busy working on her book, but I heard noises from the kitchen. Pushing open the door, I found Becky at her big floor mixer. I waited until she turned it off.

"Making more burger buns?" I asked.

"The café has been busy, and Gran keeps asking for more. I'm glad I have this great kitchen to work in."

I willed my breathing to return to normal. "What did Gran do if she ran out of buns before you came to work here?"

Becky used to share the café's kitchen with Gran, but she had only been able to do her baking early in the morning.

"She would run out, but hopefully not until closing time. She warns the customers that once the buns are gone, they're gone."

"She could send someone to the store, couldn't she?"

"Not Gran. If it isn't homemade, she isn't going to serve it."

Becky lifted the bowl onto the work counter and covered it with a plastic lid, then turned to me.

"What did you find out at the photo shop?"

"You won't believe it." I poured myself a glass of water, working to steady the tremors in my hand.

Becky leaned on the prep counter. "Okay, spill it. What did you find out?"

"Tyrone is definitely in town."

"You saw him?"

I nodded. "And there's another guy with him."

"I wonder why he hasn't been in to see Gran, yet. He has breakfast there whenever he's in town."

"Becky, he's mixed up in this drug business."

"What?"

I told her what I had overheard. "And Cal isn't available. He had to go to help with an accident or something."

"This next shipment is supposed to come tomorrow?" she asked.

"That's what Sean said. And then he's leaving town."

"The police are on to the drugs coming in through the art gallery." She reached for her own cup of water. "It seems like he'd have already left."

"Maybe he thinks the police are assuming that, too. This last shipment must be worth the risk."

"Do you think he's the one who killed Caro?"

I drank some water while I thought it over. "I don't know. He threatened Tyrone with a knife, not poison. He seems to think she died of natural causes."

"He could have been lying, right? Who would admit to committing murder?"

"A killer who thinks he wouldn't be caught." I rubbed my temples. "It doesn't add up."

"Well, we know one thing. Sean and Tyrone are using both sides of the old school building to smuggle drugs. Cal needs to know."

I pulled out my phone and speed-dialed Cal's number. It rang a few times, then went to voice mail.

"Cal, this is Emma. I need to talk to you. Call me when you can."

I closed out the call and leaned my chin in my hands. Becky mimicked my stance on the other side of the prep counter.

"Have you had lunch yet?" she asked.

"I don't want any lunch. I want someone to tell me what to do."

"I'll tell you what to do. You need to eat. Feed those little gray cells."

I glanced at the clock on the wall. It was past noon. "Maybe you're right." I heard Rose's door open and Thatcher trotting toward the door. "And maybe we need someone with new ideas."

Becky grinned. "I've got some chicken salad in the cooler. I'll fix sandwiches while you grab Rose."

Within a few minutes we were gathered at one of the dining room tables with our sandwiches. Thatcher settled himself on the floor between Rose and me.

While I ran through the morning's events, Rose listened, her gaze focused on the far wall. By the time I finished, her sandwich was gone, and she pushed her plate aside.

"First, I saw the accident that pulled Cal away on the news. It's a large one near Keystone. Thankfully, no one was killed, but there are quite a few injuries."

"Do they know what caused it?" Becky asked.

"Patchy fog. It was a chain-reaction accident involving more than a dozen cars. Cal is going to be tied up all day." Rose stirred sugar into her tea. "Second, if that last shipment isn't supposed to arrive until tomorrow, we have time."

"Do you think we should call someone else? Cal isn't the only person in the sheriff's department," I said.

"What evidence do we have?"

I pushed my own plate away, my sandwich only half-eaten. "None. CSU cleared the scene after the break-in, and there's no evidence left."

"All we have is a conversation you overheard."

"And that's just hearsay. The police would need more evidence before investigating, wouldn't they?"

"Cal would investigate with that little bit of information," Becky said.

"And we have time to wait for him." Rose sipped her tea, the fragile cup cradled in her capable hands.

My aunt's calm demeanor washed over me. "I left a message on his phone, so he'll call when he gets a chance."

Rose nodded. "I wouldn't worry too much until you hear from Cal."

We spent the rest of our lunch time discussing the inn and the guests who were arriving next week, then Rose got up from the table.

"I'm going to get back to my writing. I'll see you this afternoon." Thatcher didn't budge. Rose patted her leg. "Come, Thatcher. It's time to go back to the office."

"You can leave him with me," I said. "I'll take him for a walk."

After Rose went into her suite, I helped Becky clear the lunch dishes while Thatcher sprawled on his side under the table.

"A walk?" she asked.

"I have to do something. It won't take me long to clean the guest rooms, and I need to work out this case. A walk is what I need."

"You're still thinking about Caro's and Mike's deaths, aren't you?"

I closed the dishwasher as Becky spread oil on the prep counter and turned the bread dough out.

"I can't figure out how their deaths work into this drug deal. Sean doesn't seem to be the type to use something as subtle as poison."

"Don't do anything foolish," she called after me as I left the kitchen.

I finished cleaning the guest rooms in record time. While I was in the Walker's room, the bottle of nicotine spray mocked me from the bedside table. I had been certain the nicotine was the key to this puzzle, but it didn't fit at all with what I had overheard this morning. The whole situation was an irritating twist that was giving me a headache. I needed some fresh air.

Thatcher followed me outside and we headed up Graves' Gulch Road. I hadn't been up this way all week. I took a deep, mind-clearing breath as I climbed up the slope to the trail leading to the mine. The corgi ran ahead of me as I turned, following the trail past the mine and up to the overlook. In spite of the memories associated with this place, it had become my favorite thinking spot. I sat on a boulder far from the precipice and looked out over the open canyon to the mountains beyond.

I checked my phone to see if Cal had returned my call while I had been out of cell range, but there was nothing. Thatcher hunted for chipmunks as I replayed the morning's events in my mind.

Nothing made sense.

One clue trail led to Sean and Tyrone and the drug

smuggling. Caro had been involved, and Cal had the theory that Mike had witnessed something on his way to the ice cream social. That would involve Sean also. But what about the nicotine on the picture frames in both deaths? And the timeline didn't fit. Mike hadn't been home to handle the picture between the time he walked through the alley and when he died.

The other trail led to Debbie Walker. Even though the evidence against her was flimsy, Debbie had the means, the motive, and the opportunity to kill Caro. And didn't they always say poison was a woman's weapon?

But where did Mike fit into that trail?

Thatcher came back to me, panting and unsuccessful in his hunt.

I pulled him up to my lap. "Hey, buddy. No chipmunks today? Sorry." I rubbed his ears. "You'll have to be patient and wait for them to come out again."

He perked up at a rustle in the underbrush behind us and jumped down, ready to investigate.

I yearned for clues as much as Thatcher yearned to chase those chippies. As I watched him nose around the bearberry shrubs, an idea formed. If I hadn't heard from Cal by this evening, I could stake out the alleyway behind the photo shop. Sean had been vague in the timing of the last shipment's arrival - what if it came and went before morning? Someone needed to be there to witness it.

I stood up and brushed bits of the granite boulder from my seat.

That someone would be me.

Fifteen

Taylor stopped at the reception desk when her family returned to the inn for afternoon tea. I had just finished confirming another reservation for September.

"Hi, Taylor. How was your day?"

"It was okay, but today is Friday."

I caught the downcast look. "And you're leaving tomorrow, aren't you?"

"Yeah. Our vacation is over." She watched her family sit at one of the tables, Toni's plate piled high with scones. "I sure like it here."

"Maybe you'll be able to return next year."

"Mom and Dad talked about that, but they also said we should visit another place. I think Mom wants to go to Hawaii."

"That would be fun." I tried to sound encouraging, but Taylor wasn't in the mood.

"How will I know how the mystery turns out? Who murdered those two people?" She leaned toward me. "What have you found out? Any new clues?"

Tons of them. But nothing I could share with Taylor.

"The clues all lead to a case Deputy Cal is working

on, and I promised him I'd back off until he solves it. Maybe he'll have more information for us tomorrow."

"But I won't be here then. I won't know what happens."

"Tell you what." I took one of the inn's business cards and pointed out the inn's email address. "If your mom and dad say you can, email the inn after you get home, and I'll send you an update on the case."

Taylor took the card. "But I hate not seeing it through to the end. What if you need my help to solve the puzzle?"

"You have been a huge help already."

"It isn't the same." She sounded miserable.

"You could solve mysteries at home."

"Nothing ever happens there. No murders or anything."

"Mysteries don't have to be murders. Maybe one of your neighbors has had their mail stolen, or someone has lost a cat. There are puzzles everywhere." I smiled at her. "Nancy Drew never ran out of mysteries to solve."

"Well, maybe."

"Things will work out. You'll find your mysteries."

She smiled back. "Maybe I'll be the next Nancy Drew, and Toni can be my sidekick."

"See? Ideas are forming already."

The Thomas family weren't the only ones leaving the next day. Violet and Charles were checking out, as well as Dave and Joy Albert. The Walkers and the Brooks sisters were planning to leave on Sunday.

I spent the rest of the afternoon finishing up the accounts for the guests who were leaving and making notes about the next guests coming in on Saturday evening and Sunday. Another full house next week. When everyone had left for supper and their evening plans, Becky found me.

"Where have you been all afternoon?"

I closed the computer program. "Working. It's the changing of the guard tomorrow."

"That's right. Has Cal called yet?"

I checked my phone, even though it hadn't rung in the five minutes since the last time I had checked it.

"Not yet. I'm beginning to wonder if he got my message?"

Becky opened an app on her phone. "The news says the highway is still closed, so we know Cal is busy. Let's get some supper in town. Want to grab a sandwich at Pete's or get a pizza?"

"I've had enough pizza this week. Let's go to Pete's."

Rose had come out of her suite. She was dressed to kill in a black sequin-covered sheath dress. "Did I hear you girls are going out for supper?"

"We thought we'd head to town." I indicated her dress. "You look like you have plans."

She glanced in the mirror by the front door and fluffed her hair. "I'm off to a fundraiser in Rapid City and will probably be gone until midnight. Someone will need to stay here to welcome the guests back." She gave me a pointed look.

"You're right." I turned to Becky. "Get some sandwiches from Pete's and we'll eat them here. I'll stay and babysit the inn."

"Thank you, Emma." Rose gave me a quick kiss on the cheek then headed down the hall to the garage. "Bye, girls. Don't wait up."

Supper was fun. Becky and I ate in her apartment while Tim prowled around the unfamiliar space and Thatcher watched every bite we took. We watched a couple episodes of a British mystery show until after eight o'clock, then Becky stretched.

"It's my bedtime."

"And it's time for me to head downstairs. The guests will be returning soon." I picked up Tim. "See you in the morning."

"I hope we hear from Cal by then." Becky yawned. "Let me know, okay?"

"Sure thing." I carried Tim to my suite, then went downstairs, Thatcher on my heels.

I greeted the guests as they came in. The Brooks sisters stopped at the beverage bar to make cups of herbal tea.

"How was the Mammoth Site?" I asked them.

"Wonderful," said Sally Marie. "And so interesting. We spent the entire afternoon there."

"You didn't get too tired, did you?"

"I feel right as rain."

Betty Ann pulled a stuffed toy out of a shopping bag. "I bought a mammoth to keep our buffalo company."

"The neighbor children at home like to play with Betty Ann's toys," Sally Marie said. "She always buys new ones on our trips."

"It's like heaven on earth to have those children visit, isn't it." Betty Ann sighed. "It must be time to go home. I'm missing them like a hound dog misses his supper."

"We have one more day, and we had better get some sleep."

"What are your plans for tomorrow?" I asked.

"Back to Custer State Park," Sally Marie said. "We wanted to go to Sylvan Lake. We ordered a picnic lunch from that sandwich place in town, and we'll spend the whole day there."

"And rent a paddle boat," said her sister. "Doesn't that sound like fun?"

By ten o'clock everyone was home except Rose. I was done babysitting the Sweetbrier, and Cal hadn't called.

It was time for me to head to the art gallery for my stakeout. I laughed at myself. A stakeout? All I planned to do was to keep an eye on the alley.

I looked at Thatcher, sacked out at my feet. I could put him to bed in Rose's suite, but his company would be welcome tonight. I left a note for Becky and Rose, in case they wondered where we were, then snapped Thatcher's leash on. I grabbed a sweater since the nights in the mountains were chilly and headed to town.

At ten-thirty Paragon was quiet. All the businesses were closed except for Hogs and Suds and the convenience store at the other end of Main Street. I led Thatcher around to the alley behind the old photo shop. No one was there, either, although I had seen a light on the second floor.

I turned on my phone's flashlight just long enough to find an overturned plastic bucket between the dumpster and the wall. Shivering a little in the cool air, I lifted Thatcher onto my lap.

"Okay, buddy." I helped him settle in so his pointy feet didn't dig into my legs. "Now we wait."

Thatcher soon tired of my lap and jumped down to investigate the smells around the dumpster. I stood up and hugged myself. It was chillier than I thought it would be. I checked my phone. Ten-forty-five. This night was going to last forever.

After another thirty minutes I was beginning to question whether this was a good idea or not. Thatcher had given up his investigations and was asleep at my feet. Nothing was going on in the alley, and even Hogs and Suds had closed. The night was so still that I heard an owl hooting in the forest beyond the church. The alley was awash with the light of the waxing gibbous moon rising above the hills in the east.

When my phone vibrated, I jumped. Thatcher raised his head until I pulled my phone out, then relaxed again when I opened Cal's text.

Your message sounded urgent. Text me when you get this.

Cal was all business.

I called him. When he picked up, I kept my voice as low as I could.

"I have some news about Tyrone. He has a partner. A last shipment of drugs is coming sometime tomorrow."

"Why aren't you asleep?"

"I'm watching the alley in case the delivery comes early."

"A stakeout? You and Becky?"

"I'm with Thatcher. Becky is at home."

"I'll be right there."

Ten minutes later I heard tires crunch on gravel. Thatcher growled low in his throat until he recognized Cal.

"You probably need this." He handed me a cup of c-store coffee and pulled another overturned bucket next to mine, setting a white paper bag on the ground.

"Now, tell me what's going on."

I took a deep breath. He wasn't going to be happy when he heard about my adventure. I told him everything.

He scrubbed his face with his free hand. "I should arrest you for interfering with an investigation."

I turned my cup in my hands. The hot Styrofoam warmed my cold fingers.

"But the details you heard were valuable." He gave me a light jostle with his elbow. "I don't know how else we would have learned what's going on."

"You're not angry with me?"

"No. Not angry." He scrubbed his face again. "You put yourself in danger. Do you know what they might have done to you if they had caught you? We already knew Sean was involved when we found his fingerprints. He's bad news." He scooted closer to me and put a warm arm around my shoulders. "I don't know what I'd do if anything happened to you."

I let myself melt into the folds of his leather jacket. "But I'm okay. They didn't know I was there."

"Only by the grace of God." He sat up and lifted the paper bag. "I brought fuel for the stakeout."

He opened it and I reached inside.

I laughed when I grabbed a donut and pulled it out. "Really? I thought cops and donuts were only a stereotype."

He pulled out his own donut. "Caffeine and sugar keep me awake during long hours on the job better than anything else."

The donut was delicious. "How did you get here so quickly? Is the accident all cleared up?"

"Yup. The only injuries were minor, but there was a mess to clean up and reports to write. I got home about eleven, then sent you the text. I figured you'd be sound asleep, and I'd hear from you in the morning."

"All I could think about was that the delivery would come in the early hours, and we'd miss it."

"What were you planning to do?"

"I figured I could at least get a license plate number and a description of the suspects."

His phone pinged. "It's Rose, wondering if I know where you are." He texted back.

"She must have gotten home from her date."

Cal finished off his donut. "Rose? On a date?"

"She didn't call it that. She said she was going to a fundraiser, but you don't wear a sequined black dress for a fundraiser, do you?"

He chuckled. "I wouldn't. But to this fundraiser, she would. Tonight was the annual Mount Rushmore League dinner. A fancy affair. Everyone from local society people to the Governor was there."

"Oh." Once again, I realized how little I knew of Rose's life.

We sat in silence for a long time. I finished my cold coffee and checked the time on my phone. Two-fifteen. The moon was directly above us.

A light appeared on the second floor of the building.

Cal leaned close and whispered, "Whatever happens, you stay here and keep Thatcher quiet."

"What are you going to do?"

"Take care of things."

A few minutes later, the sound of a truck approaching on the highway reached us. I heard it downshift, then turn onto Willow Street, drive past Gran's Café, and into the alley.

The door at the back of the photo shop opened and Sean was silhouetted in the light from the back room. While the truck parked, Cal radioed for backup.

The truck's driver killed the lights and the engine. I picked up Thatcher and backed into the shadows behind the dumpster. When the corgi growled low in his throat, I shushed him.

"We need to keep quiet," I whispered in his ear.

He licked my chin, then watched Cal.

Sean walked to the back of the truck as the driver raised the door with a loud clatter.

"Where's Caro?" he asked. The driver was a heavy-set, middle-aged man.

"She's out of the picture. Had a heart attack last week."

"That's too bad." With a grunt the driver climbed into the back of the truck. "I've got ten boxes for Caro. My orders are to deliver them to either her or Tyrone Jackson." He turned toward Sean with a shotgun in his hands. "And you aren't Tyrone." He racked the slide on the gun.

The faint sound of a siren in the distance distracted both men. Cal stepped out from the shadow of the dumpster, his hand on his service revolver ready to draw.

"Police. Both of you freeze."

The next moment, everything seemed to happen at once. The guy in the truck turned in Cal's direction. Moonlight glinted blue-black on the barrel. Cal dodged to one side as the shotgun went off. Sean dove into the photo shop's backroom, and Thatcher launched himself in Sean's direction.

I ran after Thatcher, past Cal, who had grabbed

the shotgun barrel and pulled the guy out of the truck and had him face down on the ground.

Sean was kicking at a ferocious corgi who was attacking his legs. Thatcher had brought him to the ground and wasn't letting up. I called on my self-defense training and put my knee on Sean's back, pinning him to the ground, and twisted his arms behind his back.

Just then two more sheriffs' vehicles pulled up, one from each end of the alley, sirens on and lights strobing the darkness. Help had arrived.

By the time Cal dropped me off at the inn, I only had an hour to catch a nap before I needed to get up. I set my alarm for five o'clock and snuggled with Thatcher on my couch.

But every time I closed my eyes, the only thing I could see was that blue-black shotgun barrel pointed right at Cal. Now that the adrenaline had worn off, all I could think about was how close I had come to losing him.

He was arrogant, determined, opinionated...and incredibly sweet.

I wasn't falling for the man, though.

I wasn't.

My alarm woke me up in time for a quick shower and to take Thatcher out for his morning potty break. After he did his business, I stumbled into the kitchen, more than ready for my first cup of coffee.

Becky frowned at me. "I saw your note. What do you mean by going out on a case without me?"

I sipped the hot coffee. "I was only going to

watch, and you needed your sleep. I know what time you have to get up in the morning."

"Um hm," she said, putting one hand on her hip and sounding like a character from one of my favorite television mysteries. "I got up in time to hear you close your door."

"Shh." I held up one hand as I sipped my coffee again. Thatcher had chosen a spot in the corner of the kitchen and was already sound asleep. Lucky dog.

"Who were you watching all that time?"

"I was waiting for that delivery Sean had spoken about. It was our last chance to close down the drug ring."

"Um hm. And that's why I saw Cal's SUV leave here at four o'clock?"

"Yeah. He joined me on the stake-out. He brought donuts."

"Um hm." Her hand was still on her hip.

I rubbed my temples. "Why do I think you don't believe me?"

"I'm just trying to protect my cousin's reputation. Out at all hours of the night with a beautiful woman? Gran would have his hide if she knew."

"You're not worried about my reputation?"

She pointed a spatula at me. "You don't have to answer to Gran."

"We had a chaperone. Thatcher was there."

"Um hm."

"Would you stop saying that? Cal arrested the bad guys. He brought me home as soon as he could afterward."

Becky dropped her spatula. "You mean you were serious? The case is closed?"

"It is if they're the ones who killed Caro and

Mike."

My phone vibrated. Cal.

"Hey, Cal. What's up?"

"We finished questioning Sean, Tyrone, and Dale." His voice sounded like he was as wiped out as I was.

"Dale?"

"The truck driver."

Oh, yeah. The guy with the gun.

"What crimes are you charging them with?"

"Not murder. Sean and Tyrone were still in Arizona when Caro died, and in Colorado when Mike died."

"What about Dale?"

"Can't make it stick. He was in Washington State, with receipts to prove it."

I drummed my fingers on the counter. "Then who killed Caro?"

"I'm calling it natural causes. Mike, too. We've wrapped up the drug investigation and we can't pin murder on these guys. No murder, no suspects. Case closed."

"It's too much of a coincidence." My head ached in the way that only a good night's sleep could fix. I finished my coffee and walked over to the counter to pour a second cup. "Both people dying of the same cause with nicotine in their system? And nicotine found on the picture in Sally Marie's room?"

"Let me sleep on it. You should, too. We both had a short night."

"I have guests checking out this morning. I'll take a nap later."

I closed out the call and sipped my coffee. The caffeine was beginning to kick in.

Becky pulled a muffin tin full of cinnamon

goodness out of the oven. "You look like you've hit a dead end. Did I hear Cal say the case was closed?"

"Yeah." I leaned on the end of the prep counter as Becky set the muffins on a cooling rack. "What are those?"

"Bread pudding muffins."

"And the paper cups? They look like mountain peaks."

"They're called tulip liners. I decided to use brown to go with the cinnamon in the recipe."

"They're fancy. Like something you'd find in an up-scale restaurant."

She gave me a sideways look. "That's the idea." She went to the freezer and pulled out a bowl of fruit slush.

"That stuff doesn't have a fancy name, but the guests certainly liked it last week."

"I decided to serve it in crystal stemware this morning. Make it fancy in spite of the name." She stirred the half-frozen slush with a spoon. "But you're trying to change the subject. Who is the murderer?" She dropped her voice to a hissing whisper. "What about Debbie Walker? The one with the means, motive, and opportunity? Just because Caro wasn't killed by her drug-running friends doesn't mean someone else didn't do her in."

"I hate to think Debbie is a cold-hearted murderer."

"Did those kinds of feelings ever stop Miss Marple?" She took four pieces of cut-glass stemware out of the cooler and started spooning slush into them. "If you think Caro was murdered, and if Cal is sure the drug gang didn't do it, then the murderer is still around here somewhere."

I poured myself a third cup of coffee. "But the question is where? And who is it?"

"That's two questions."

I left to set up the dining room.

The Thomas family had asked if they could have an early breakfast since they needed to leave for the airport at seven. Becky had their bread pudding muffins and fruit cups ready for them when they came downstairs.

Taylor and Toni both looked miserable.

"Cheer up," I said. "You'll soon be home and you can see all your friends again."

"It won't be the same," Taylor said. "They haven't experienced what we have. They'll be all, 'Sure, Taylor, trees and stuff. Just wait until you see the new guy. What new clothes are you buying for school in the fall? Want to go hang out at the skate park?' And I don't care about any of that stuff anymore." She shot a glance at her parents who were already eating their breakfast.

"I want Mom and Dad to move here," said Toni. "I found the perfect house to buy. It's only a few miles down the road." She shoved her hands in her pockets. "But they said they have to go back to their jobs on Monday. Boring jobs."

"Jobs that pay the bills," I said. "You know, living here isn't the same as it is when you're here on vacation. People here have jobs and go to school. The house still needs to be cleaned and sometimes it can be as boring as anywhere else."

Toni gave me a skeptical look and went to join Terri and Ted.

"Kids." Taylor shook her head. "She's so unrealistic. What jobs would Mom and Dad get if we moved here? Dad's company doesn't have an office here and Mom just got a promotion."

"It sounds like you've given it some thought, too."

She twirled one of her curls around her finger. "Yeah. I have. I think when I grow up, I'm going to look for a job I can do in a place like this. Mom and Dad brought us here because they wanted us to experience life away from the city. It worked. I really like it here."

"It sounds like a plan to work on. By the way, Deputy Cal made some arrests last night."

"Is the case closed? What happened?"

"Some people were transporting drugs through the art gallery. They won't be doing that anymore."

"But what about the murders? Who killed Caro and Mike?"

Violet and Charles came out of their suite. They greeted the Thomas family as Charles parked the wheelchair next to a table and went to the beverage counter to make their morning tea.

"The police think the deaths were from natural causes after all."

Taylor's eyes narrowed. "You don't believe that do you?" It was more of a statement than a question.

"For now, it seems I have to. All the evidence points in that direction. And those guys the deputy arrested are bad news. I'm glad they're in jail."

After breakfast, we said our goodbyes. Terri and Ted lingered behind after the girls wheeled their suitcases out to the car.

"Can we make another reservation?" Terri asked.

"We would love to have you back again. Sometime next summer?"

Ted exchanged glances with his wife. "We were

hoping for the first week of October. The girls have a long weekend for fall break." He cleared his throat. "It will be a surprise for them."

I grinned, thinking of how ecstatic the girls would be, and how much fun it would be to see them again.

"Of course, and I won't spoil it."

Dave and Joy Albert were just as enthusiastic when they checked out.

"We're going to coordinate with the Walkers for our next visit. We'll let you know."

I pulled the luggage cart over to Charles and Violet's suite when they were ready to go and helped Charles load the suitcases on.

Rose pushed Violet's wheelchair out to their van. "We're glad you chose the Sweetbrier Inn for your vacation," she said.

"We enjoyed it." Charles turned to look at his wife. "Didn't we, Violet?"

The poor woman looked tired, as if she hadn't slept well the night before.

"Did you get to do everything you wanted to in the area?" asked Rose.

Violet spoke as if through gritted teeth. "Not everything."

"You'll have to come back sometime, then."

Violet didn't answer as Charles loaded her wheelchair into the van through the accessible side door. I put their suitcases into the back, then stood with Rose as they drove away.

"They didn't seem very happy as they left," Rose said. "I wonder what else Violet wanted to do?"

"It must be something in Paragon," I said. "They didn't turn at the highway but went into town."

We returned to the dining room where the

Walkers were sitting at a table with the Brooks sisters.

"I've been wanting to do some sketching," Debbie was saying, "and Rick wants to try fly fishing. Jack at the sports store in town let him rent some equipment and we're going to spend the day at Deerfield Lake."

"We're going to a lake, too," said Sally Marie. "What a coincidence! But we won't be fishing."

"Paddle boats," said Betty Ann. Her face beamed like she had invented the boats herself. "We'll go boating on the water like we did when we were girls. Do you remember, Sally Marie? Aunt Letty had one shaped like a swan."

Letty? The name pushed against the fog in my brain.

Sally Marie picked up where Betty Ann left off. "All of our aunts and our mama were named for flowers." She ticked the names off on her fingers. "Daisy, Pansy." She stopped and nodded to Betty Ann. "That was Mama. Then there were Violet and Hyacinth."

Debbie looked confused. "Where does your Aunt Letty fit in? Isn't Letty short for Letitia?"

Sally Marie giggled. "No. It's short for Violet. Aunt Letty never liked being named after a flower, so she went by Letty her whole life."

My mind cleared as if a fresh breeze had blown through it. I turned to Rose. "I need to go to town. Call Cal and ask him to meet me at the art gallery as soon as he can."

Sixteen

The streets of Paragon were still quiet just past eight o'clock in the morning. I paused on the corner outside Gran's Café and peered down Main Street. No white van. I ignored the aroma of bacon frying that drifted through the café's open door and crossed the street. There was only one place they could be.

The alley behind the photo shop didn't look too different than it had the night before except for the crime scene tape and the white van parked outside the door to the art gallery. It must have been Charles who had laid planks on the stairway to allow access for Violet's wheelchair. The padlock the police had used to secure the door had been snapped and the door stood open.

I crept up the planks and into the back room. From the art gallery I could hear voices. Charles's held a pleading tone. And was Violet crying?

I moved closer, careful not to let them see me. Now I could distinguish what they were saying.

"Violet, it's over. It's over."

Peeking in, I saw Violet standing at the painting on the wall, clinging to the frame to keep herself upright.

Violet ran her hands over the paint - in a caress? No. She was scratching at it with her fingernails. Tearing it. All the while, her wrenching sobs filled the air. She turned to the desk behind her and grabbed a letter opener. With it she stabbed and stabbed at the painting.

"It's mine," she sobbed. "She ruined it. Ruined everything." Stabbing over and over. "Where is *Debut de Printemps*? Where is it?" Now strips of canvas were falling away from the painting revealing the wall behind it.

I couldn't stand any more.

"Stop, stop." I ran to her, grabbing her arm. "You're destroying Caro's painting."

Violet turned on me, hatred distorting her face. "Caro's painting?" Her voice was a screech. "Caro's painting?" She stabbed at the ruined canvas again. "She stole my masterpiece. She destroyed it…" The words trailed away as her strength gave out.

Charles caught Violet as she collapsed and eased her into the wheelchair. The woman's sobs were deep and wracking.

"Caro Lewis ruined my lovely painting."

The letter opener dropped to the floor.

"What do you mean?"

I glanced at Charles, but he didn't say anything. He only stood next to her chair, his face distorted in misery.

Touching Violet's arm, I tried to get her to answer. "How did Caro ruin your painting? This is Caro's painting, isn't it?"

"She stole my *Debut de Printemps*." I recoiled at the hatred in Violet's voice. "She took the only thing I had left in my life after the accident and destroyed it."

"You mean Caro didn't paint this picture?"

"She took credit for it, but it isn't hers. It was never hers."

Violet grasped a dangling ribbon of canvas and ripped it down. She rubbed at it, and flakes of green paint fell off, revealing the dusky purple of the painting from the photograph on the academy's website.

"You are Letty Carmichael, aren't you?"

The sobs had dissolved into shudders. She clung to the scrap of canvas. "That was a long time ago."

"After the accident, when it looked like you wouldn't survive, Caro claimed that your painting was hers and added her own touches."

Violet snarled. "She destroyed it. I should have won the Highspring Award, but Caro…" Her voice failed as she crumpled the canvas strip in her hand.

"You killed Caro for revenge. But why did you wait so long?"

Violet waved me away. Charles took a handkerchief from his pocket and wiped the tears from his wife's face with a tender motion.

His eyes met mine, then he looked back at his wife. He tried to soothe her, pulling her close in an embrace, but she pushed him away.

"It's over, Violet," he said, his voice steady. "It's all over now."

His tender words calmed her. She sat quietly, although her hands still trembled. I heard someone at the back door.

"Emma?" It was Cal. "Are you here?"

Violet clung to Charles. "You know what you have to do," she said, gazing into his eyes.

He seemed to have her under control, so I met Cal

in the back room.

"It's Violet. She's in there."

Cal's eyes went wide, then he pushed past me into the gallery.

Charles and Violet were just as I had left them. He had his handkerchief in his hand and was wiping her mouth. Such tender care showed his love for her.

"What's going on here?" Cal asked. He looked at the wall. "Who destroyed the painting?"

"Do you want me to tell him?" I asked Charles.

He nodded, his arms around his wife.

"It all started nearly fifty years ago," I said. "Back when Violet Bishop was known as Letty Carmichael."

Violet watched me. A slight smile had changed her into a beautiful woman. Letty Carmichael refined by fire and grief.

"Letty and Caro were friends. The best of friends. But at the same time, they were fierce competitors. And as much as Caro tried to deny it, Letty had that rare strain of talent most artists can only dream of. It can't be taught, and all the practice in the world can't make it appear. It's something you're born with."

Violet nodded her head in agreement. She closed her eyes as she listened to the story she knew all too well.

"Letty and Caro were both working on their senior projects at Forestgreen Academy of Art, and they were almost finished. Both chose the same subject, the coming of spring. Caro called hers *Almost Spring*, while Letty named her masterpiece *Debut de Printemps*. The same name in English and in French. It would be the last painting Letty ever did. Before the paintings were finished, she was in a horrific car accident. Everyone thought Letty would die from her injuries, and she almost did. Isn't that right, Charles?"

He nodded.

"I'm not too clear about the next part," I said. "You met Letty in the hospital where you worked as a pharmacist?"

"That's right." Charles crouched next to Violet's chair and took her hand. "I fell in love. Once she recovered, we were married."

"But her recovery took months, didn't it?"

"Years." Charles brushed Violet's hair away from her forehead. "But I didn't mind. She was beautiful, and she was mine. We've had a happy life together, haven't we, dear?"

Violet leaned against him. She must have expended all her strength destroying the painting.

"I'm not sure about the next part, either. At some point, probably within the last year, you saw an article in a magazine or newspaper about Caro?"

Charles nodded. "It was last fall. *Contemporary Artist* did a story on what promising young artists of the past fifty years were doing now, and Caro was on the cover. I had never met her, but Violet recognized her right away."

"And in the article was a photo of Caro's prize-winning *Almost Spring*.

A tear trickled down Charles' cheek. "That was how it started. Violet became obsessed with finding Caro. She had recognized *Debut de Printemps* immediately. That's when she learned Caro had taken her painting, changed the colors to the ones she had used on her project, and claimed Violet's work for her own."

Cal broke in. "You mean, this painting isn't Caro's?"

"No. Caro must have destroyed her own painting and substituted Violet's. No one noticed." Charles patted Violet's hand, then held it in his own.

"Except Violet," I said.

"Except Violet."

"When did she decide to kill Caro?"

That startled Cal. He shot a glance at me.

"I'm not sure." Charles brushed Violet's hair back again with his free hand. She looked like she had fallen asleep. "She came to me with the idea in January. She had it all worked out. She needed me to help her determine which poison to use, how to administer it, how strong of a dosage to use." He sighed. "And she had the plan to poison several other objects so others would fall ill. But she didn't want anyone else to die." He cleared his throat. "That was very important to her."

"But it all fell apart when Mike died."

More tears fell. "No one else was supposed to get hurt. She knew some would feel sick, but they wouldn't die. Only Caro."

Violet let out a deep breath, then there was silence.

No. No. No.

"Cal." My voice trembled. "Violet. Look at Violet. I think she's stopped breathing."

Charles still clung to his wife's hand as Cal checked her pulse.

"What did you give her?" I asked Charles. Panic made my voice strident.

"She wanted to die the same way we had killed Caro. Silently. Without fuss."

"The handkerchief. You wiped her mouth and there was nicotine on the handkerchief."

Charles nodded. His expression was sad. So sad.

He pulled the handkerchief from his breast pocket along with a broken spray bottle. The source of the nicotine. He dropped both into a plastic bag Cal pulled out of his pocket.

Cal stepped back, sealing the bag. "You know I have to arrest you for murder."

"Please," Charles said. "Can you leave me alone with her? Only for a little while? I want to say goodbye."

His voice was tight, and tears flowed down his face.

"We'll wait outside."

I followed Cal out into the alley.

"I can't believe he poisoned her while we were there, and we missed it."

Cal ran a hand through his dark curly hair. "I missed it. I should have realized what he was doing."

"Can you believe that sweet couple was behind the murders?"

"I have to admit it, Emma. You were right."

"Except I wasn't. I never suspected Violet." I turned to look back into the art gallery. "And Charles. He helped her every step of the way."

"Charles-"

Cal ran back into the gallery. Charles was slumped against Violet's chair, still grasping his wife's hand. He looked up as we ran in.

I started breathing again. It would have been so easy for him to take his own life, too.

Cal called for an ambulance.

The next afternoon, Rose and I sat on the inn's

front porch with tall glasses of raspberry lemonade. Two more glasses sat on the side table waiting for Becky and Cal.

"Such a sad ending to Violet's life," Rose said. "And Charles. He'll spend the rest of his life in prison."

"I never would have thought they would be capable of such evil." I stirred my drink with my straw.

"We're all capable of evil. It's only by grace that we escape the same fate as Charles and Violet."

"It all started with Caro, didn't it?" I watched the butterflies flit between the flowers in the rock garden. "She took credit for Letty's painting."

"This particular episode did," Rose said. "But I'm sure the roots of these deaths started long before Caro and Letty met in school. They were both broken people, with no one to bring healing to their lives."

I sipped my lemonade as I watched Cal's SUV drive up Graves' Gulch Road and pull into the inn's driveway. He and Becky joined us on the porch.

"Thanks for the lemonade," Becky said as she sat next to Rose. "I thought we'd never get done at Gran's. Birthday parties take forever."

"Didn't you have a family birthday party last month?" I handed the last glass of lemonade to Cal as he sat next to me on the wicker love seat.

"We have one every month that someone has a birthday." Cal took a long drink. "Today we celebrated all the June birthdays."

"How many are there this month?" Rose asked.

"Three." Becky counted them off on her fingers. "Jeremy is turning nine, Shasta is turning twenty, and Cal-"

"Let's just say I'm older than either one of them," he growled.

"Emma's birthday is in June, too," Rose said.

Becky jumped on her comment. "Oh, which day?"

Rose smiled. "The twenty-ninth. The same day as Cal's."

"We'll have to have a party for them!"

"Calm down, Becky," I said. "I'm busy that day. Rose has given me the day off and I have plans."

"Well, I guess we could have a party for Cal."

"No can do." Cal crossed his ankle over his knee and extended his arm along the back of the love seat. "I have plans that day, too."

"Rats. I was hoping you'd ask me to make a birthday cake for you."

A car turned up Graves' Gulch Road and drove slowly toward us.

"That looks like it might be our new guests," Rose said. I started to get up, but she stopped me. "You and Cal relax. You've both had a busy weekend. Becky and I can handle this."

As they went into the inn, Cal's arm moved from the back of the love seat to my shoulders.

"I thought they'd never leave." He fingered the fabric of my t-shirt's shoulder. "You didn't tell me you had plans for the twenty-ninth."

"I was just thinking ahead. I plan to take the day off, but I haven't decided what I want to do yet."

"I think you should climb Black Elk Peak."

"I've been wanting to do that. It's the highest mountain in the Black Hills, isn't it?"

"Over seven thousand feet. The tallest mountain between the Rockies and the Pyrenees."

I took a sip of my lemonade as the new guests

walked by.

"Why should I climb it that day?"

"Because I do it on my birthday every year, and I thought it would be nice to have company this time."

"That actually sounds like a good idea."

"I have them sometimes." He cleared his throat. "But it's almost a month until then. We should do something together while we wait."

"Like what?"

"I know a nice restaurant in Hill City."

"I remember you saying something about that before."

"You're torturing me, Emma."

I sipped my lemonade. I had never had this much fun teasing anyone before.

He cleared his throat again. "Would you have dinner with me?"

"When?"

"We had better make it tonight."

"Why?"

He shifted in his seat to look directly into my eyes. "Because with you around, things tend to happen to change my plans."

I grinned. "Tonight is good. Is it a date?"

"It's a date."

AUTHOR'S NOTE

This second book in The Sweetbrier Inn Mysteries was so much fun to write. I enjoyed moving Emma and Cal along in their on-again/off-again romance as well as showing Emma and Becky take their places as permanent staff members of the Sweetbrier Inn.

I want to thank my husband for his invaluable input into this story. Several times a day I'll interrupt his tasks to ask him about a detail or two in the narrative. He's also more than willing to accompany me on forays into the Black Hills for "research," otherwise known as going on a hike through the back country.

I also need to thank Beth Jamison of Jamison Editing for her work on this project, and Hannah Linder of Hannah Linder Designs for the wonderful cover.

Keep an eye out for more Sweetbrier Inn Mysteries to come! A Christmas novella, *A Wintertime Tale*, is currently on my computer, and I hope to bring you the third Sweetbrier Mystery in the spring of 2023.

You can keep up with all of my writing adventures by subscribing to my newsletter. Just head over to my website, www.JanDrexler.com

And find me on my Facebook page, www.facebook.com/JanDrexlerAuthor

Recipes

Becky's Summer Celebration French Toast

ingredients:
8 thick slices of bread
2 eggs, beaten
2 cups milk
2 teaspoons vanilla extract
1/2 teaspoon ground cinnamon
butter
2 cups fresh raspberries (or strawberries)
2 cups fresh blueberries
4 ounces cream cheese, softened to room temperature
2 cups confectioner's sugar, reserving about 1/4 cup for the final step
2-4 Tablespoons of milk

Make glaze: Beat the cream cheese in a small bowl until smooth. Add the confectioner's sugar a little at a time, alternating with milk, until you have a liquid glaze that will be easy to pour.

Prepare fruit: Wash the fresh fruit and drain.

Preheat oven: On warm setting, or about 250°.

Prepare the French Toast:

Preheat a griddle or frying pan to medium heat and melt the butter.

In a medium bowl, whisk the eggs, milk, vanilla, and cinnamon together. Pour the egg mixture into a flat 8" x 8" baking dish. Dip the slices of bread into the mixture, allowing them to absorb some of the liquid, then turn the bread over to coat the other side in a similar fashion.

Cook until the slices are browned on both sides, about 5 minutes. Place the cooked slices on a baking pan and place them in the oven to keep them warm until you're ready to assemble the plates.

Assemble the plates:

Cut each slice of French Toast into two triangles and arrange them on a plate with the peaks pointing up.

Drizzle the glaze over the French Toast, then scatter the fruit over and between the slices, letting it spill onto the edges of the plate.

Liberally sprinkle the reserved confectioner's sugar over each plate.

Serve immediately.

English Sausage Rolls

ingredients:
1 puff pastry sheet, or pie crust for a single-crust pie
12 ounces mild pork sausage
herbs to add into the meat (optional): thyme, sage, or onion
1 egg & water mixture for egg wash

Preheat oven to 400° and line a baking sheet with parchment paper.

In a small bowl, whisk together the egg and water. Set aside.

On a floured bread board or other work surface, prepare your pastry. If using puff pastry, divide the dough into thirds and use one third for each rectangle (commercial puff pastry comes folded in thirds.) If using pie crust pastry, roll it into a rectangle. The rectangles for either kind of pastry should be about 12" long and 4" wide, and you will need three rectangles.

Prepare the meat: Add any seasonings you desire, and divide the meat into thirds. Roll each third into a log about 12" long.

Place one log in the center of one pastry rectangle. Fold the pastry over the log. Before sealing the edges, brush a bit of the egg wash along the edge. Overlap the pastry edges and press the edges down with a fork to seal them together. Repeat with the other two logs and rectangles.

Using a knife, score the pastry with lines along the top or the roll, about 1/3" to 1/2" apart. Cut the sausage rolls into slices about 1-1/2" thick. Place them on a baking sheet, spacing them evenly. Brush the tops with the remaining egg wash.

Bake the sausage rolls in a 400° oven for about 20 minutes, or until golden brown. Transfer them onto a wire rack to cool.

Veva's Amish Fruit Slush

ingredients:

2 cups sugar

3 cups boiling water

1 (12 ounce) can frozen orange juice concentrate

6 large bananas

1 (20 ounce) can crushed pineapple

18 ounces 7-Up or other sparkling clear beverage

Fresh fruit for garnish: peaches, grapes, or berries

In a large bowl, dissolve the sugar in the boiling water. Add orange juice concentrate, bananas, and pineapple. Stir in the 7-Up, then pour into a large bowl.

Freeze.

Before serving, thaw at room temperature, stirring occasionally, about one hour, or until slushy.

Serve in bowls or cups with fresh fruit to garnish.

Books by Jan Drexler

The Sweetbrier Inn Mysteries

The Sign of the Calico Quartz

The Case of the Artist's Mistake

A Wintertime Tale (coming November 2022)

The Amish of Weaver's Creek series

The Sound of Distant Thunder

The Roll of the Drums

Softly Blows the Bugle

The Journey to Pleasant Prairie series

Hannah's Choice

Mattie's Pledge

Naomi's Hope

Novella

An Amish Christmas Recipe Box from *An Amish Christmas Kitchen* collection

Books from Love Inspired

The Prodigal Son Returns

A Mother for His Children

A Home for His Family

An Amish Courtship

The Amish Nanny's Sweetheart

Convenient Amish Proposal

About the author

Jan Drexler lives in the Black Hills of South Dakota where she enjoys hiking and spending time with her husband and their expanding family. She has published several historical novels, including the award-winning *Mattie's Pledge*, and also enjoys writing cozy mysteries.

You can find out more about Jan on her website, www.JanDrexler.com

Coming Soon!

A Wintertime Tale

A Sweetbrier Inn Christmas Novella

Expected November 2022

A Wintertime Tale

One

The Sweetbrier Inn took on a special cozy atmosphere in the winter. I sipped my hot chocolate as I watched the snow swirl in the early December air outside.

"I could get used to this."

Becky, the inn's cook and my best friend, grinned at me from the leather couch. "You mean no guests, no cleaning, no cooking?"

"That's right. Nothing to do for the next four months but read the latest mystery, snuggle with Tim and Thatcher, and visit with you and Rose."

I took another sip of the rich chocolate, mentally reviewing my first summer at the inn as Aunt Rose's partner and the inn's manager. The pleasant experience had been marred by a few murders, but solving those murders had been incredibly satisfying. The inn was now closed for the winter season and I was ready to relax.

"Don't forget the Christmas tree hunt." Becky checked her phone. "We need to meet Cal up on Cloud Creek Road in thirty minutes."

I squirreled myself further into the depths of the knitted throw Rose kept on the back of the chair and watched the fire through the glass doors of the fireplace insert.

"Why don't we buy a tree? It would be a lot easier, wouldn't it?" I scratched Tim, my black cat, under the chin.

"Easier, schmeasier. Hunting for our Christmas tree in the forest is tradition." Becky grabbed my hand and pulled me up, ignoring Tim's meow of indignation as he was dumped off my lap. "It's time to go. It's going to take us twenty minutes to walk to the meeting place and you don't have your boots on yet."

I had purchased winter gear from Come on Up, the sporting goods store in Paragon, before Jack and Shasta had moved south for the winter. Becky had helped me choose sturdy boots, a winter parka, ski pants and serviceable gloves with a matching hat. The hat was her only concession to style.

"Not that hat," she said, snatching it off my head.

"Wait! Why not?"

She pulled two bright orange knitted caps out of the bin next to the coat rack in the garage. "Because it's hunting season."

"But I like that hat." Orange wasn't my best color.

"You like not getting shot more, don't you?"

I pulled the cap on.

We set off with Thatcher, Rose's tricolor corgi, who wore a bright orange bandanna around his neck. I kept him on his leash until we crossed the highway, then let him run ahead of us. Becky turned up Cloud Creek Road after we passed the church, and we headed out of town.

"Where does Cal live, anyway?"

The snow hadn't been plowed on this road, and

we walked in the tire tracks of Cal's SUV.

"Up here about a quarter of a mile. The place is called Graves' Hole. It's been in the family for almost a hundred years."

"Graves' Hole? What is it? A cave?"

"Of course not. It's a cabin set back in the trees. I wouldn't want to live there alone, but Cal says it's perfect for him."

Cal met us at the end of his driveway. He had an ax in one hand and a pack on his back. For once, he wasn't wearing his deputy sheriff's uniform. I sucked in a breath as he grinned at me, his face ruddy under his fur hat with an orange bandanna tied around it.

"Good morning. Are you ready to hunt some Christmas trees?"

Grizzly Adams. I was dating Grizzly Adams.

"We sure are," said Becky. "I know right where I want to look."

Cal gave his cousin an exasperated look. "In Jasper Canyon again? We hunted there last year and the year before."

"And the year before that. We're familiar with that area, and there are plenty of trees."

"All small ones. We've pretty much hunted that grove out. I thought we'd head into Cloud Canyon. There should be some pretty trees along the creek."

"Not there." Becky was adamant.

"You're not scared of that old story, are you?"

I stamped my feet. Now that we had stopped walking, my toes were getting cold.

"What old story?" I asked.

"Stumpy started it years ago to keep kids away from his favorite hunting grounds," Cal said as he picked up his ax again.

He started up the road, making his own trail. No one had been this way since the last snowfall.

I followed him, but Becky didn't budge.

"You don't know that story isn't true," she said, her voice echoing as she called after us.

Thatcher was ahead of me, plowing his way through the snow behind Cal.

"What story?" I asked again. "Why is Becky so afraid?"

"It's just a story about a creature who is supposed to live in the canyon."

"What kind of creature?" I glanced back. Becky had given up and was following us.

"Our own Bigfoot, according to Stumpy. Becky thinks it eats little kids for breakfast."

I looked at the thick forest surrounding us. Yeah. I could see Bigfoot haunting these woods.

I waited for Becky to catch up. "You really think Bigfoot lives up here?"

"Okay, maybe not Bigfoot. But it's something." Becky glanced around at the surrounding trees. "I thought I saw it once. Big, shaped like a man, covered with fur. I haven't been in Cloud Canyon since then."

Cal turned around at that. He shifted the ax he was carrying on his shoulder and gave me a wink.

"You know that's just a story Stumpy made up. He didn't want you kids chasing away his game."

"Then what did I see?"

Cal turned around and resumed walking up the unplowed road. "It was probably just a cat."

I ran after him. "A cat? You mean a mountain lion? Why is that better than...than Bigfoot, or whatever it is?"

"You know I like to give Becky a hard time.

There's nothing up there to be scared of. Sure, there are mountain lions in the Hills, but we'll keep them away just by all the noise we make. You'll need to keep Thatcher close by, though. He'd be a tasty treat for one of them."

Thatcher was sticking to me as if he understood the danger of exploring on his own. I agreed with him. The possibility of running into a mountain lion was enough to send me back to the inn, besides whatever it was Becky had seen when she was younger.

"Are you coming?" Cal frowned at me. "Or has Becky's story got you spooked?"

The wind blew some snow out of the tree branches above and it fell between us.

"I think I'll wait for Becky."

Cal shrugged. "Suit yourself." He continued up the road.

"Are you okay?" I asked when she caught up with me.

"Yeah. The canyon gives me the heebie-jeebies, but I'll be okay. It's just my imagination, right?"

"Sure."

My voice sounded a lot braver than I felt. The road we were on followed Cloud Creek up into the hills. The slopes rising above us were covered with trees and granite outcroppings, a mountain lion's favorite terrain for hunting. I shivered.

We left the road a few minutes later, following Cloud Creek as it led us into a narrow canyon. Cal had already crossed the stream, using stepping stones to get over, but Becky pointed to a narrow path on our side of the water.

"Let's follow this deer trail. I don't want to risk

getting my feet wet."

I eyed the icy creek bank. "I'm right behind you."

"So, what's going on with you and Cal?"

"What do you mean?"

"It isn't like him to go off on his own without you."

"I'm just not at home in the woods as much as he'd like for me to be."

"The camping trip was fun, wasn't it?"

Several of us had spent the night in the forest in October, and it had been a new experience for me.

"It was a lot of fun until the owl hooted."

Becky started giggling. "And then the coyotes! I thought you were going to die of fright."

"It isn't funny." I was still embarrassed about it. "I can handle facing an irate customer at a classy hotel, but coyotes? They slink in the shadows so you can't see them, and they make that awful noise. You can't blame me for screaming a little."

She snorted. "A little? It was like a horror movie scream." She giggled again. "There was nothing to be scared of. They were just being coyotes."

"But everyone laughed. You, Ashley." My voice dropped. "Even Cal."

Becky stopped walking and faced me. "That's it, isn't it? You're ashamed of being scared in front of Cal."

"And then he had to mention mountain lions back there, and it all came back. How can I go out with a guy that's so different than I am?"

"Keep thinking about the things you have in common. Give it some time. Maybe you'll even learn to like hearing the coyotes howl."

I shook my head as we started walking along the

trail again. "I don't think Cal will ever invite me on a camping trip again."

We picked our way over tree branches and around old stumps with Thatcher trotting between us. Across the creek, I could see Cal's bright orange bandanna as he walked up the canyon on his side and ahead of us.

"What kind of tree are we looking for?" I asked Becky, ignoring the orange beacon that bobbed in and out of the trees. "Those Ponderosa pines are big enough, but they don't look like Christmas trees."

"We want the Black Hills spruce." She pointed to the side of the trail. "There's one, but it's too small."

The tree was cute, but only about a foot tall. I heard a cry above me and looked up to see a crow flying over us, followed by a couple of his friends. They certainly didn't help my mood.

"Tell me about the time you thought you saw Bigfoot," I said as we continued walking. "Maybe we can figure out what it really was."

"It's worth a try." Becky stopped and looked around. "It was somewhere close to here. I was in fifth grade and we were supposed to collect things for the nature table at school."

"I remember doing that at my school," I said. "We collected leaves and caterpillars and things like that every fall in elementary school."

"Yup. Anyway, I came up this way and found a bunch of stuff. Even the skeleton of a deer, with the bones bleached white. It was so cool."

"And a little creepy?"

"A lot creepy. I was going around this huge pine

tree, picking up pine cones, and I saw Bigfoot, or whatever it was."

"Could it have been a mountain lion, like Cal said?"

She shook her head. "It was as tall as a man and covered in fur."

"A bear?"

"There aren't any bears in the Black Hills. At least, not usually. And it didn't have a snout like a bear or a wolf has."

"Did it make any noise?"

"That's why Gran thought it was just my imagination. It didn't make any noise at all. It didn't even move. I just took one look, dropped the bag of things I had collected, and ran home to Gran's."

"It must have been a bush or a tree."

"Nope. No way."

"Why are you so certain?"

Becky's eyes held mine. "Because the next morning, I found my bag of nature stuff. Someone had left it on the back step during the night."

"Are you sure it wasn't Stumpy that you saw? Didn't you tell me he spends his time hunting for stuff like that in the forest?"

She shook her head again. "I would have known if it was Stumpy. He's a lot shorter than whatever it was I had seen. And he always wears that cowboy hat. I would have recognized him."

The wind picked up and the sunshine disappeared. Clouds were moving in.

"We had better find our Christmas tree," Becky said. "It's already three o'clock and we want to get home before dark."

We had only walked another five minutes or so

when I spotted a perfectly shaped tree.

"Let's look at that one up there." I started up the hill.

We were both puffing when we reached it. Thatcher sniffed in the snow around the base as I looked up to the top far above us.

"Too big," Becky said. "Rose wants one around ten feet tall for the inn."

"So now we're Goldilocks? One is too small, one is too big."

"We'll find the one that's just right. Look down there, by the creek."

Down the hill was a thick grove of spruce trees. In the center of the smaller trees was a huge one that had fallen recently. The roots, still covered with soil, stuck up into the air.

"Let's look there," Becky said. "We might find one in that bunch."

We slid down the slope. Becky started walking around the edge of the grove, but I was captured by the size of the tree that had fallen. I pushed my way to the trunk. It was at least thirty inches thick. Much larger than the smaller trees surrounding it. Thatcher was with me as I made my way around the trunk to the roots. When the tree had fallen, it had left a wide hole in the bank of the creek. Snow filled the cave-like opening.

Thatcher sniffed, tunneling with his nose as he went. He moved closer to the edge of the depression, his tail wagging. Then suddenly he froze, quivering. He jumped back, barking at the opening his nose had made.

I couldn't see signs of anything alive. No tracks or anything. But Thatcher kept barking at the snowy hole. I picked up a stick and poked at it, enlarging the opening. Suddenly the snow fell into the deep pit. Inside, in a dark recess tucked far under the tree roots, was a skull. A human skull.

"Emma?" Cal's voice drifted from the other side of the creek. "Are you all right? What is Thatcher barking at?"

The skull stared at me.

"I think I found Becky's Bigfoot."

And it had been there for a long time.

Made in the USA
Middletown, DE
05 June 2023

32132088R00163